# SECRET AGENT "X" IN
# LEGION OF THE LIVING DEAD

From nowhere hurtled that black death car. And from nowhere came its grisly occupants. They were not of the earth, for their human flesh was immune to bullets. They were not of the grave, for they manned the wheel and a blasting machine gun . . . Secret Agent "X" made a desperate maneuver to block their invasion of the land of the living. And in that weird terror trap, he came face to face with a man he knew — a man he knew had died five years ago.

## WILDSIDE PULP CLASSICS

*The Blind Spot*, by Austin Hall and Homer Eon Flint
*Far Below & Other Horrors*, edited by Robert Weinberg
*The Golden Dolphin*, by J. Allan Dunn
*The Grand Cham*, by Harold Lamb
*Murgunstruum and Others*, by Hugh B. Cave
*Out of the Wreck*, by Captain A.E. Dingle

## BY JOHNSTON MCCULLEY

*Black Star*
*The Mark of Zorro*
*The Spider Strain and Other Tales*
*Tales of Thubway Tham*

## BY ROBERT E. HOWARD

*The Complete Action Stories*
*Gates of Empire*
*Graveyard Rats*
*Treasures of Tartary*
*Waterfront Fists*

## PULP MAGAZINE FACSIMILES

*Strange Tales* #7 (January 1933)
*Ghost Stories* (June 1931)
*Spicy Mystery Stories* (August 1935)
*Spicy Mystery Stories* (February 1937)

## THE MYSTERIOUS WU FANG

*The Case of the Suicide Tomb*, by Robert J. Hogan

## OPERATOR #5

*Blood Reign of the Dictator*, by Curtis Steele

## SECRET AGENT "X"

*Legion of the Living Dead*, by Brant House

# SECRET AGENT "X" IN
# LEGION OF THE LIVING DEAD

## BRANT HOUSE

**WILDSIDE PRESS**

**LEGION OF THE LIVING DEAD**

Originally published in *Secret Agent "X"* Magazine
Volume 6, Number 2 (September 1935).

This edition copyright © 2004 by Wildside Press.
All rights reserved.

Published by:

Wildside Press
www.wildsidepress.com

# I
## HELL ON WHEELS

IT was an afternoon in late spring and from a cloudless sky, the sun beat shimmering rays on the stream of motor cars that flowed sluggishly along the narrow canyon between the rows of tall buildings. Along the sidewalks, men and women, many of them richly attired, hurried about their business and pleasure. It was a street of wealth, a main stem of American finance.

But the men and women in the street seemed oblivious to the criminal monster who preyed like a vampire upon this veritable artery of wealth. Had they noticed the faces of the men in the great black touring car that cruised along slowly with the traffic, they might have lost some of their sense of security. For these men were grim-faced police — one of many specially picked squadrons that had been patrolling the streets day and night, waiting for the radio call to duty — and probably to their own destruction.

The man at the wheel of the squad car was young for a position that involved so much responsibility. His face told of many anxious moments, of the torment of trying to fathom the unfathomable. He steered the car without apparent effort, yet his every nerve was keyed to a high pitch. His brilliant eyes strained ahead; yet sometimes sought the rear vision mirror, watching for that with which human forces seemed powerless to cope.

Suddenly, from the radio speaker came the voice of the police announcer. At the first word, the driver of the squad car detected a different note in the man's voice. The drab monotone was gone; rather the announcer's voice was colored with a tremor of excitement and dread. He was exercising his duty in transmitting the message that had come to him, but he seemed to know that in doing so he was sending some of his companions to their doom.

"Special cruiser twenty-four . . . Calling special cruiser twenty-four," came from the loudspeaker. "Proceed at once to the Krausman store. Robbery going on. Robbery going on at Krausman store . . . Number one-three . . . Number one-three."

The last group of figures was simply a code which the department used to identify the activities of a mysterious criminal gang which had terrorized the city with daring thefts accompanied by what amounted to nothing short of wholesale butchery.

As the driver of the squad car set his siren going, another very human appeal came from the radio loudspeaker. For a moment, the vast police organization was forgotten. It was simply one anxious father speaking to his son: "For the love of God, watch your step, Jimmy!"

The jaw of the young man at the wheel of the squad car was thrust far forward, as his foot came down heavily upon the accelerator. The police announcer was an elderly man who had been pronounced unfit for active service. It was his son who manned the wheel of Special Cruiser Twenty-four. Duty had made heavy demands upon father and son. The anxiety of the father could well be imagined. He might just as well have pronounced his own son's death sentence.

A wide lane in the traffic appeared miraculously before the speeding, screaming squad car. The police sat on the edge of the cushions. Their knuckles whitened as they clenched the butts of heavy revolvers. Now and again one of the men would send a strained glance back through the rear window.

Suddenly, the man beside the young driver pinched his companion's arm.

"It's coming!" His voice was hard and brittle, strained to the breaking point. The driver's lower jaw protruded a bit more. He uttered a heartening oath through clenched teeth. His eyes flashed upward toward the rear vision mirror. The stretch of cleared street behind them was broken by a sinister blot of speeding destruction. A long-nosed streamlined roadster, black as midnight, was rapidly overhauling them.

THE police car was still three blocks from the scene of the robbery and the car behind them seemed to have no speed limit. Nor did the driver of the black roadster have any compassion for human life. The police cruiser swerved sharply to avoid hitting a careless pedestrian. A split second later, the black roadster bore down upon the frightened man. The pedestrian became panic stricken, put out both arms in a ridiculously futile effort to halt the speeding car, and in the next moment was knocked flat — a piteous blot that lay deathly still on the pavement.

The roadster was within a few feet of the squad car. Through the rear window, the police could see the two men crouched low and motionless in the cockpit. With a dexterous yank on the wheel, the driver of the police car sent the cruiser far to the left, trying to block off the black speed demon. But the driver of the roadster was a match for any man. As the police car swerved to the left, the roadster swung to the right. With a sudden almost unbelievable burst of speed, the roadster pulled alongside. The ugly black snout of a machine gun protruded over the door of the racer.

"Let 'em have it!" shouted a policeman. He leaned out so far that he almost touched the black destroyer. His revolver blasted at the noxious face of the man at the wheel. At such short range he couldn't have missed.

The staccato voice of the machine gun shattered the roar of the two overtaxed motors. Leaden hell raked the police cruiser from stem to stern. One policeman, who had been daringly balanced far out over the door of the car, pitched over the side and beneath the grinding wheels of the black juggernaut. The young driver jerked suddenly upright. A slug had drilled his chest. His teeth ground together with a nerve-shattering sound that he never heard.

The steering wheel spun in his hands, completely out of control. His pain-taut right leg crammed every ounce of gas into the powerful motor. The police car broke into a rubber-burning skid, careened across the street, caromed against a car, hurtled over the curb, to crush innocent bystanders beneath its bounding wheels. Screams from a hundred throats filled the street with terrific clamor. The police cruiser slammed broadside through the glass window of a department store and crumpled against a solid wall, a mass of wreckage.

But the roar of the black roadster dinned in the distance. Though the driver had received at least two shots that would have ordinarily proved fatal, the car sped unerringly onward in its mad flight of destruction, to disappear up an alley some blocks away.

Hysterical screams, frantic cries for help, drowned out the groans of the maimed that the killers' car had left in its wake. The sidewalk was strewn with corpses. Hoarse-voiced traffic police battled their way through the panicky throng toward the wreckage in front of the department store. A policeman, who had been thrown from the wrecked car, struggled to his feet. Both of his hands clutched at his side, in an instinctive but hopeless effort to stanch the blood that flowed from a jagged wound. He tottered forward to fall at the feet of a traffic policeman.

The traffic cop knelt. His arms went about the shoulders of the fallen man. His fingers clenched tightly as if he hoped by some superhuman effort to check the ebbing life. The wounded man opened his eyes and recognized the man who held him.

"Fergeson," came his husky whisper, "that — that

man in that roadster! The man with the machine gun. I shot him — shot right through him. He was Mack O'Brien's big gunman. He was Slash Carmody in the flesh!"

The traffic policeman stared incredulously at the wounded man. For Slash Carmody, killer formally employed by one of the underworld barons, had died in the electric chair in Sing Sing not more than forty-eight hours ago.

TWO blocks farther up the street from the point of the police car disaster was the famous Krausman Jewelry Store. A few minutes before the police cruiser had received its instructions to proceed to the jeweler's, Mr. Peter Krausman was sitting in his office, placidly smoking a thick, mahogany-colored cigar. He was a large, swarthy-skinned man with an unpleasantly crooked nose. Replacing his somber Oxford-gray garments with something brighter, and adding the flash of gold rings bobbing at the lobes of his ears, an artist would have had a perfect model for a Gypsy king.

Yet while Krausman seemed to be basking in the security of his own wealth, his impassiveness was a mere pose. Every nerve fiber within his body tingled in anticipation of action. His heart throbbed with slow, steady strokes; his mighty brain dwelt upon but one problem — a problem only remotely related to the jewelry business.

Through the glass window of his office door, he watched a pleasant-faced, redheaded man who was trying, clumsily enough, to sell a fine jade bracelet to a strange, dark-complexioned man with a pinpoint moustache and a long, stringy goatee. The dark man was famous throughout the city. He was Dr. Jules Planchard, a skilled plastic surgeon. Other clerks, more experienced, looked askance at the redheaded man. Obviously, the snap judgment of Krausman had failed for once. The redhead was certainly no salesman. Would he allow so valuable a customer as Jules Planchard to go out empty handed?

Planchard, however, seemed to have made up his mind as to what he wanted. He glanced at his wristwatch, waved toward the jade bracelet and ordered the redhead to wrap it up. He paid for the bracelet, thrust it into his pocket and left the store.

The redheaded clerk turned his attention to a pretty young girl who had just asked to look at wristwatches. In the office, Peter Krausman chuckled grimly. The redhead was much less interested in his attractive customer than he was in keeping half an eye on the front door.

Suddenly, the humor vanished from the swarthy face of Peter Krausman. He was watching the right hand of the redheaded clerk. It had been resting on the glass top of the counter. Suddenly, it snapped upward, and drummed twice on the counter. Krausman sprang to his feet, started toward the door of the office. Beyond, he could see the flashing body of a beautifully appointed sedan that had come to a stop in front of the store. The redheaded clerk shot a glance at the office, seized the young woman who had been contemplating the purchase of a wristwatch. In spite of her vehement protestations, he pushed her back behind the counter, and through a small door in the wall.

A fellow clerk, inclined toward gallantry, stepped in front of the redhead. The redheaded man gave the intruder a vigorous push.

"Watch your step, everybody!" his voice rang out imperatively. "It's a stickup!"

At the same moment that Peter Krausman catapulted through the door of his office, four men barged through the front door. They were men whose right hands were thrust deeply into coat pockets that failed entirely to disguise the shape of the automatics that they held. They were men whose unmasked faces were sharp with ratlike cunning. Deathly pallid faces they were, faces out of the past, faces of men who had figured prominently in old police records until death had chalked them from the list of public enemies.

Even the alert mind of Krausman, who had been prepared for something of the sort, was for a moment stunned by the appearance of these gunmen. He recognized them to a man. Every one a hardened criminal, but every face the face of a corpse.

"Everybody back against the wall," the raucous voice of the foremost member of the gang commanded. By the livid welt on his left cheek, Krausman recognized him as "Scar" Fassler, a criminal who five years ago had been pronounced dead by the prison officials who had removed his body from the electric chair.

OUTSIDE the store, a police whistle sounded. A stalwart, blue-coated figure sprang through the door. Scar Fassler wheeled about. His automatic nosed from his pocket. The policeman dared not fire, for the scar-faced gunman had taken a strategic position directly in front of the group of clerks which the gunman had herded back against the wall. He had the policeman entirely at his mercy, and for a moment he paused, enjoying his advantage.

Suddenly, Krausman, who had been covered by criminal guns as soon as he entered the room, displayed remarkable courage and agility. He sprang straight toward the gunman who threatened him. The gun in the criminal's pocket coughed, but Krausman was unchecked. His gnarled right fist drove straight into the face of the surprised criminal. The blow fairly lifted the man from his feet, but even before he had struck the floor, Krausman had hurled himself upon Scar Fassler. Fassler sent one hurried shot at the policeman in the doorway, turned, and fired point-blank at Krausman.

The shot struck Krausman, and for an instant he tottered. But it was only a ruse. In seeming to fall forward,

Krausman's legs shot out like two springs of steel, launching him in a flying tackle. His broad shoulder struck Fassler's knees. The corpse-faced gunman tried to spring backward out of the way of Krausman's clawing fingers. But the jeweler seized Fassler by the ankle.

The gunman crashed to the floor, twisted over, and kicked Krausman in the head with his hard left shoe. For a moment the hold on the gunman's ankle relaxed. Fassler sprang to his feet with an oath. His gun swung around, this time aimed at the jeweler's head.

Though on the floor, groggy from Fassler's cruel kick, Krausman must have realized the peril of his position. The two shots that had already stuck him had been rendered ineffectual by the bulletproof vest he wore. Fassler knew this. This time, he would shoot for the jeweler's head.

A shot rang out. But it was not from Fassler's gun. Krausman's redheaded clerk, who had been engaged in a hand to hand conflict with one of the mobsters, had discovered his employer's peril. The redhead had suddenly drawn a gun from his pocket, and tried a snap shot that struck the barrel of Fassler's automatic. The gun was knocked from the mobster's hand. Deprived of his weapon, Scar Fassler's small piggish eyes filled with terror.

"It's a trap, boys!" he shouted. He sprang toward the redhead whose well-placed shot had saved Krausman's life. Fassler's was the courage of a cornered rat. He ignored the sudden threatening forward thrust of the redhead's gun.

"No, Jim! Don't shoot!"

It was Mr. Krausman who had shouted this warning to the redheaded man. Krausman knew that panic possessed Fassler, that the mere sight of a gun would not halt him. But he must be taken alive, if a man who had died in the electric chair could ever again be called alive.

The redhead heard his employer's warning, and held his fire. Fassler swung with his left, a long fast blow that the redhead failed to duck. The man called Jim staggered back against a counter. Krausman had pulled himself to his feet, and was coming toward Fassler with a gun in his hand. Fassler shot a glance toward the door. His companions had beat a hasty retreat as soon as he had uttered his warning. Instead of making toward the front door as Krausman evidently expected him to, the scar-faced gunman sprang back toward the office.

Krausman had recovered his agility. He ran in the same direction that Fassler had taken. The criminal sprang through the door of the office, slammed it, and twisted the key in the lock. Krausman backstepped, hunched his shoulder, and drove like a battering-ram at the door. Tenons of the door squawled apart under the power behind Krausman's heavy shoulder, but the door held. Krausman's right shoe came up in a kick that shattered the door glass. Disregarding the cutting fragments of glass that still adhered to the frame, Krausman straddled the frame and in another moment was in the office.

But a second door had opened and closed behind Fassler — the door into Mr. Krausman's shower and lavatory. Krausman believed that Fassler was trapped. A heave from his powerful shoulder burst open the bolt of the door. The door sprang open, and Krausman, gun in hand, stood in the room, looking bewilderedly about him.

Fassler, the scar-faced gunman, who for five years had been officially dead, had apparently vanished like a ghost.

His swarthy brow deeply furrowed, Krausman stared about the room. He walked over and opened the frosted glass door of the shower. Empty. He turned to a small linen-closet and opened it. Again he had drawn blank. But no — What was that square of blackness at one end of the closet? Krausman took a small fountain-pen flashlight from his pocket and switched on its needlelike ray. The light showed a large square hole that had been cut in the wall. It revealed the water pipes that led to the shower bath. Had this hole been left open in order to make the shower pipes accessible for repairs?

The alert mind behind the swarthy face of Peter Krausman had suggested a double purpose in this opening. He reached out his hand and touched the pipes with the tips of his fingers. His keen sense of touch had detected a slight vibration in those pipes. Then he knew how Fassler had engineered his surprising escape. The opening evidently extended down into the basement of the building. The pipes, had they been placed there expressly for the purpose, could not have offered a better means of descent.

But how had Fassler known of this opening? Surely he had not stumbled upon it by chance. For a moment, Krausman debated whether to follow. He decided that he wouldn't. Fassler had gone unerringly to the one rathole that had offered him a means of escape. He had evidently the advantage of knowing much more about the building than the swarthy-faced man who, to all appearances, owned it.

It was an odd situation. And for a moment amusement glinted the eyes of the man who until an hour ago had never entered the Krausman Building. But it was a situation that to some extent explained the courageous actions of the man who appeared to be a wealthy merchant, unused to violence and hand to hand encounters with criminals.

For the swarthy face of the man, who at that moment had discovered a secret exit from the building, was merely the result of clever disguise. Beneath dark-colored pigment, beneath plastic material and face plates which had counterfeited Peter Krausman's features in every detail, was a face that no living person had seen — the face of Secret Agent "X."

Acting upon a tip that had traveled the length of the underworld's grapevine telegraph, Agent "X" had taken advantage of the real Peter Krausman's absence from New York. He had deliberately impersonated the wealthy jeweler, knowing to a certainty that the most ruthless gang of robbers that he had ever encountered had planned to loot the Krausman Store.

He had staked much to frustrate the thieves' scheme. But his chief desire was to capture one of the members of the gang and thus dispel the mystery that had baffled the police. For though the idea seemed too ridiculous to warrant its publication in newspapers, the entire gang of murderous thieves seemed to be made up of criminals who had long since died. Scar Fassler was only one of a legion of corpse criminals.

Had some master scientist actually discovered the long-sought secret for reviving the dead? Had some mad doctor taken criminals, fresh from the execution room, and brought them back to life, to recruit a vast underworld army of men who, knowing death once, would not fear it a second time?

This was the riddle that Secret Agent "X" sought to solve. Wise in the way of the perverted geniuses who directed major crime groups, "X" knew that the knowledge of life eternal could be a greater scourge than all the lethal weapons that man could produce. Fear of death, he knew, was the only thing that prevented thousands of men from forsaking the law for the lawless.

# II
## GREEN EYES

TURNING from the shower room, Secret Agent "X" disguised as Krausman the jeweler, encountered the red-headed clerk who had conducted himself so courageously throughout the encounter with the criminals. His hair was a tangled mop, and his jaw was swollen.

"What happened to that scar-face?" he demanded excitedly. "I've seen that man before. He looked like a hood by the name of Fassler. But Fassler is supposed to be dead. You should have let me shoot him, Mr. Krausman."

"No, Hobart. I wanted him alive," declared Agent "X." He conducted Jim Hobart to the closet in the shower room, and showed him the hole in the floor. "That will bear investigation, Jim. I hadn't the slightest idea there was anything of that nature in here. It seems to be an avenue of escape well known to that criminal."

Frowning, Jim Hobart looked from the opening in the floor to the swarthy face of the man who had employed him. Perhaps he was thinking that it was extremely odd that Peter Krausman did not know every detail of his own office.

"Did they get much loot?" Secret Agent "X" asked of his aide.

Hobart shook his head. "But that policeman was badly wounded. One of your customers, a Mr. Stinehope, was knocked out. That's about all at this end of the line."

"What do you mean by that?" inquired "X."

"Why, Commissioner Foster is outside there now with a group of police and he told me that the officer who was shot got in an alarm before he entered the store. One of those special squad cars was on its way here when they encountered that mysterious black roadster with the mounted machine gun — the car that's been made so much of in the papers."

"X" seized Hobart by the arm. "Did it —"[1]

Hobart's nod interrupted him. "The police car was completely wrecked. Only one of the men is expected to recover. No clues at all as to the mystery car. In fact, the mystery has deepened. It seems that the sole survivor of the police car wreck insists that he got in several shots at the driver of the death car. Two of the shots went home, he is certain. Yet the car steered unerringly on its course, the machine gun spitting death."

"Maybe the driver of the black roadster wore a bulletproof vest," the Agent suggested, "just as you and I did."

Hobart nodded. "Possible, of course. But this cop, who's expected to pull through, swears that he sent a bullet straight through the forehead of the driver of the mystery car. The driver didn't so much as budge, he says. What is more, the cop recognized the man as Slash Carmody — who was executed in Sing Sing only a day or so ago."

Frowning, Agent "X" turned toward the door of the office. On the other side of the broken glass, he saw a grave-faced man of medium height whom he recognized

---

[1] AUTHOR'S NOTE: Followers of the "X" chronicles have probably recognized the redheaded clerk as Jim Hobart, the young man who directs the Hobart Detective agency, one of the units in the Secret Agent's vast crime fighting organization. Though the Hobart group resembles any other private detective bureau in that it is at the service of the public, Jim Hobart's first duty is toward Agent "X", who befriended him in a time of need. In as much as Hobart knew "X" only in the character of A. J. Martin, a newspaper correspondent, it is little wonder that he failed to recognize his friend when "X" adopted the identity of Peter Krausman.

immediately as Police Commissioner Foster. Foster's thin lips curved into a smile. He nodded at the man he supposed to be Krausman, opened the door and walked in.

"One of your customers informs me that you managed to frustrate this attempt to rob your store, Mr. Krausman. You are to be congratulated."

Agent "X" shrugged. "I am afraid that your praise has fallen in the wrong place, commissioner. If it hadn't been for Mr. Hobart, here, I wouldn't be talking to you at this moment."

THE police commissioner nodded at Hobart just a bit reservedly. Though the Hobart Detective Agency was rapidly making a name for itself, Foster habitually regarded all private detectives with suspicion.

Another man appeared in the office door. He was small, gray-eyed, and thoughtful looking. "X" recognized the man as one who had entered the store only a few moments before the robbery. The little man stroked thin, blond hair nervously, and glanced from Foster to "X."

"Commissioner," he said hesitantly, "what is to be done? I declare, the police make no headway against this mob of killers! Mr. Krausman has done more to check them than the police." The man opened the door of the office, and approached "X" with his thin right hand extended. "I would like to shake your hand, sir. Stinehope is my name."

Agent "X" took Stinehope's limp hand. Stinehope was a name that had been famous in the banking world. For the past year, however, the bank which Stinehope had directed had been closed. Nevertheless, little Mr. Stinehope seemed to retain an envied position in the realm of finance.

Commissioner Foster winced slightly. "I am sure we all commend Mr. Krausman most highly, Mr. Stinehope.

However, we can all feel somewhat relieved. The police force is about to be firmly reinforced by one of the greatest criminologists this city has known. I had a long talk with my old friend and former superior, Major Derrick. Derrick, you will remember, was the police commissioner who retired in my favor some time ago. He has promised to give us every assistance. He should be here by now."

Stinehope nodded thoughtfully. "Ah, yes. I remember Derrick. Splendid man, he was. A hard worker; a straight thinker. No offense intended, Foster."

"X" said nothing, thoughtfully studied Stinehope.

"And now, Mr. Krausman," said Foster, "can you give us a description of some of the men who took part in this attempted looting of your store?"

Agent "X" frowned. "Perhaps I can. I think there were four of them. That right, Hobart?"

"The leader," Agent "X" continued, "had a long scar down his left cheek — or perhaps it was his right."

He knew that it would not do for him to give too accurate a description. In the character he was playing, he would not be expected to show as much accuracy in matters of detail as a trained criminologist would.

Commissioner Foster fumbled in his pocket and brought out a picture. "This the man?" he asked. He handed the picture to "X."

The Secret Agent took the picture. It was indeed the photograph of the supposedly dead Scar Fassler. He nodded slowly. "Undoubtedly, that is the man."

At that moment, the door of the office snapped open. A wiry, blond little man who seemed a bundle of nerves stepped into the room. He jerked a birdlike glance from first one to another of the men in the room. The nostrils of his little nose spread, and he inhaled quickly and noisily as if he were taking snuff.

"Foster!" he rapped.

The commissioner turned, a smile lighting his usually grave face. He seized the newcomer's hand, began pumping it up and down. "Major Derrick! You're just in time to help us out!"

"Glad to, glad to," Derrick sputtered. He nodded at Stinehope. "Hello, hello." He turned on "X," looked him up and down. "Mr. Krausman, I suppose. Hello. Most unfortunate circumstances." He sniffed sharply.

"Derrick," said Foster, "Mr. Krausman has positively identified the man who led this mob as Scar Fassler!"

Turning abruptly to "X," Derrick rapped out: "And what would Mr. Krausman say if I told him I saw Fassler executed in the electric chair five years ago?"

Agent "X" regarded the blond Lt. Major Derrick for a moment. "I would be inclined to say that one of us had made a mistake."

"Possible, possible," Derrick whipped out. "But I don't make mistakes of that sort, Mr. Krausman. And, I might add, you do not appear to me as a man who makes mistakes."

"How does it happen that you were prepared for this holdup, Mr. Krausman?" asked Stinehope curiously.

Agent "X" laughed. "When you have half a million dollars tied up in rare gems, you don't take chances, Mr. Stinehope. I always have some one in the store to watch things. Today, it just happened to be Jim Hobart."

Foster turned to his former superior. "What would be our best first move, major?" he demanded.

Derrick sniffed. "Reward, first off. Post a reward for a starter. We need a responsible citizen, some one the people respect to head a committee to post a reward." His birdlike eyes jumped at Stinehope. "The very man!" his voice lashed like a whip. "Stinehope, will you head the reward committee? Advise you to make the appointment, Foster, if Stinehope will accept. And you will, eh?"

Stinehope considered a moment. Then: "Certainly. I will be glad to do anything."

"Good!" declared Foster. "Will talk with you in a

moment, Stinehope. And now, Krausman, can you give us any further information concerning the men in the criminal group?"

"X" shook his head. "I'm afraid I'm not very observant. I suggest that you interrogate Mr. Hobart. He is trained in such matters. I'm rather tired now. If you don't mind, I'll look around the store, and see if there has been much damage or anything stolen."

Without waiting for permission, "X" strode through the door of the office. He had sighted a group of news-hungry reporters, and among them a young girl. She was undeniably beautiful. From beneath her jaunty hat, he observed wisps of golden hair. Her starry eyes were deep blue. Her smart attire became her perfect figure.

As the man who looked like Peter Krausman entered the store proper, the reporters came at him in a body, waving notebooks and clamoring for permission to take pictures. "X" endured the searching rays of photoflash lamps, and then tried to get past them toward the door.

"Statement for the press, Mr. Krausman?"

"Sure, give us a story, Mr. Krausman."

"Yeah, tell us how it feels to sock a gunman."

Agent "X" smiled: "Try it yourself and get first hand information," he suggested.

"Ah, give us a break!" a young reporter appealed.

"Very well. But I dislike talking before a crowd. One of you, that young lady, perhaps — I'll see in private. She can give you all the story when I'm through."

Smiling, the golden-haired girl came forward. This was Betty Dale of the *Herald*. Little did she know that this swarthy-skinned man with the broken nose was her old friend, Secret Agent "X."[2]

---

2 AUTHOR'S NOTE: Daughter of a former member of the

"Where can we go, Mr. Krausman?" she asked.

"X" indicated a little room apart from the store proper. There were a number of similar rooms in the building. Some were used as showrooms to display gems of rarest quality to prospective buyers. Others were small offices set apart for certain members of Krausman's staff.

"Don't hold out on us, Betty," cautioned one of the reporters good naturedly as "X," steering Betty by the elbow, entered the tiny room. The Secret Agent closed the door, and quietly twisted the key in the lock. He turned toward Betty, a smile on his thick lips. If the girl wondered at his locking the door so carefully, there was no sign of alarm on her lovely face.

"Please sit down." The Agent indicated a chair behind a small walnut telephone desk. She complied with his request, spread her notebook before her, and regarded the man she believed to be Peter Krausman inquiringly.

"If you don't mind, I should like to hear the story of the robbery as you observed it, Mr. Krausman. Just when did you first realize that the store was being held up?"

"X" seated himself on the edge of the telephone desk. "I knew that it would be held up nearly ten hours ago. I really don't know just how I would have managed to be here at the exact moment, if it hadn't been that Krausman left town this morning."

Betty's white forehead crimped into a tight frown.

---

police force, it seemed a natural course of events that Betty Dale should turn to police reporting when she became old enough to select a career. Though left alone in the world, she was not without friends — many of them detectives who knew her father. But her staunchest friend, and the man she admires most, is Secret Agent "X". Together, they have encountered many perilous adventures, previously recorded. Her admiration for the Agent has grown to a beautiful, unselfish love.

"You knew it ahead of time? I — I don't quite understand."

"Then don't bother your pretty head about it any longer. Perhaps this will clarify matters for you, Betty." Secret Agent "X's" forefinger traced the letter "X" on top of the desk.

"No!" she exclaimed excitedly. She smiled happily. "I should have known! But —but I never do. I had no idea that these strange robberies were so serious as to attract your attention."[3]

"Not serious, Betty? Do you realize that in the last two weeks nearly a score of police have met death in conflict with that black car?"

"Then there is a definite connection between the mystery car and these robberies?"

"Assuredly. As soon as a robbery call goes out over the radio, that black, torpedo-shaped car puts in its appearance. With total disregard for the lives of innocent bystanders, the machine gun on the killers' car opens up. Slugs rake the squad cars hurrying to the scene of the robbery. Not once have the police reached the scene of the robbery in time to prevent the crime from being committed." The face of the man who looked like Krausman became suddenly grim. "It is the most ruthless butchery I've ever encountered! The man behind it all must be bent on wiping out the entire police force. And through it all,

---

3   AUTHOR'S NOTE: It should be explained for the benefit of those who meet the Agent for the first time herein, that though Betty Dale has met him often enough to know him probably more than any other person, she has never seen his true face. Her love for him is not based upon romantic dreams revolving about this man of mystery; it is the underlying, thoroughly human qualities of the man that attract her. For always, Agent "X" is kindly to those who merit kindness; never has he willingly harmed the defenseless. Even his enemies attest the quality of his mercy.

he remains hidden, as invisible as a black panther at midnight and far more dangerous."

"Have you any idea who the hidden criminal may be?" Betty asked.

"Not the slightest," replied "X" without hesitation.

A worried frown crossed Betty's face. "Commissioner Foster thinks he knows," she said. "I was in his office this morning when he received a mysterious note. He permitted me to make a copy. But I just can't turn it in to the *Herald*. It's too absurd!"

"May I see it?" "X" asked.

The girl reached into the pocket of her jacket, and took out a piece of paper. "It —it frightens me," she said simply as she handed the note over to "X."

The Secret Agent opened the paper and read through the letter quickly.

> Dear Foster:
>     This is an open challenge. Dare you pick up the glove? For every man who has met death at the hands of the law, I shall take the lives of ten members of the police force. A vaster army than you can muster is behind me. It is the Legion of Corpses. The secret of life eternal is mine; yet to my enemies, I mete out certain death. Dare you take up the glove?

The paper jerked almost imperceptibly in the Agent's hands. For this open challenge from the lawless to the law was signed, "Secret Agent 'X'."

"X" looked at Betty. A fear that his smile could not dispel was in her deep blue eyes. "You know what that means?" she asked. "Foster will demand your capture, alive or — or —"

The Agent laughed quietly. "There's been a price on my head before. Go ahead and publish that note in your paper. If you don't, some other paper will. It doesn't matter, anyway." He handed the piece of paper across the desk.

As Betty extended her hand for the note, her elbow knocked over the telephone. The girl uttered a startled: "Oh!" and started to recover the instrument.

Agent "X's" hand shot out and closed over her wrist. A strange change had come over his face. His eyes were like bright points of gleaming steel. Gently, he disengaged Betty's fingers from the phone, picked up the instrument, and stared at it a moment before setting it down. Then he slid from the desk, crossed the room on tiptoe, one finger on his lips. He beckoned to Betty. Wonderingly, the girl got up, and followed him. The Secret Agent put both hands on her shoulders, bent his head, and whispered into her ear:

"Go back to the desk, sit as you were sitting, and keep talking for about a minute. Then, newspaper or no newspaper, leave this office immediately. I don't want to hide from you the fact that you are in deadly danger. Avoid all strangers. Take care of yourself, but don't be afraid. Go back now." He gave her a gentle push, and turned toward the door.

AGENT "X" unlocked the door, opened it, and stepped outside. Reporters were waiting for him, eager with questions. With his back to the door, "X" inserted the key in the lock, and turned it. Then he dropped the key to the floor, found it with his heel, and kicked it under the door.

"Where's Miss Dale?" demanded one of the reporters.

"Inside," the Agent explained. "She's putting her notes in some order. Don't worry; she'll not hold out on you." Then he pushed past the reporters, turned abruptly to the left, and entered another office. It was empty. He hurried over to the desk and bent over the telephone. A moment's scrutiny told him what he wanted to know. Beneath the receiver hook of the instrument was a small wooden wedge driven far enough in to open the telephone circuit. A similar wedge he had seen on the phone in the room in which he had talked to Betty.

It was safe to wager that every phone in the building had been similarly opened so that anyone listening at any of the extension phones on the circuit might have heard his conversation with Betty Dale.

As "X" hurried from the little office he was wondering if the robbery attempt that afternoon had been the failure he had thought it to be. Perhaps there was another motive — one that spelled danger for himself — and for Betty Dale. He wondered, too, if Krausman's absence from the city that afternoon was as innocent as it appeared to be.

Avoiding Commissioner Foster and Major Derrick, who were busy with the police investigation, "X" hurried along the wall of the store, stopping at every door to look in the rooms beyond. All were empty. The police had herded all the store's employees into one group, and were busy firing questions at them.

Agent "X" turned to the back of the store, glanced into Krausman' s office, and hurried on to another room where were the vaults in which Krausman kept certain valuable jewels. The door was locked.

Taking from his pocket a bunch of master keys, without which he never ventured forth, he selected one that would fit the lock. In another moment, he was inside the room. It, too, was empty. But "X" immediately noticed the absence of the telephone which usually sat upon the desk. The phone wire itself passed beneath the slightly raised window and out into the alley.

"X" picked up a straight office chair and quietly tiptoed to the window. Raising the chair level with his chest, his arms shot out like two pistons. The chair crashed through the glass. "X" followed the chair, leaping over the sill to drop ten feet into the alley outside. Recovering his balance immediately, he glimpsed the phone swinging against the outer wall. A small window-washer's ladder leaned against the wall. But these were minor details and the matter of only a moment's observation. Near the window was a sleek, cream-colored roadster. The door was open and a woman was just stepping in. She sent one glance over her shoulder before dropping into the deep cushions.

For a moment, "X" saw her face, though partially concealed by the soft fur that trimmed the collar of her extravagantly beautiful dress. Her face was small, nearly round, and dark complexioned. Her lips, slightly voluptuous, were rouged a striking shade of red that was almost like Chinese lacquer. Her nose was slightly uptilted and her eyes were actually arresting; true emerald green, they were beneath long, penciled brows that curved upwards at the outer extremities.

But what struck Agent "X" as being extremely important was the flash of green in the bracelet about her left wrist. He was certain that the woman wore the jade bracelet that he had watched Dr. Jules Planchard purchase.

The woman's lips parted, emitting a husky, purring sort of laugh.

"X" saw that the motor of the car was running. He sprang toward it in an effort to catch hold of the spare-tire carrier, but even as he leaped, the clutch grabbed and the car scudded off down the alley.

"X" pivoted. A trim black sedan, one of the Agent's own cars, was parked directly behind the jewelry store. He made for it, sprang into the front compartment, and plugged at the starter. The motor kicked over, thrummed smoothly. He shifted gears soundlessly and gave the great supercharged motor all the gas it would take. Like a black projectile, his car shot down the alley.

Ahead of him, the woman's roadster nosed through a traffic lane, and turned to the right. "X" rounded the corner, his car whining in second gear. He cleared the broad bumper of a moving truck by a hair's breadth, purposely threw the car into a skid that shied it across the track of a speeding sedan. Ahead, the cream-colored roadster wove through traffic, putting two more cars between its tail-lamp and the nose of the Agent's car.

He accelerated, sounded his horn, and crowded the car in front of him to the curb. A comparatively clear lane ahead, the cream-colored car, with its exotic driver, pulled away. The tweet of a traffic officer's whistle was wasted on unheeding ears. The green-eyed woman could drive, and her car was capable of taking all she gave it.

"X" had seen the green-eyed woman before. Felice Vincart was her real name, but it had given place to the alias she had made famous. Snatched from the variety stage by an ardent young millionaire who had fallen in love with her, Felice Vincart had found herself a widow after a few months. In spite of her wealth, she had not gained a position in the social register. She remained known not by her husband's name but by the alias she had made famous. When the tabloids exploited her voluptuous beauty she was invariably called "The Leopard Lady."

It was an appropriate appellation; for Felice Vincart had a grace and manner that was actually feline. Her act in the theater had consisted of a wild, barbaric dance, revolving about two great leopards which she herself had trained.

How had the Leopard Lady, with all the pleasures that money could buy at her disposal, become associated with the criminal who directed the activities of the sinister corpse legion? Perhaps a life of indolence had held no thrills for the woman who had tamed jungle beasts.

Agent "X" had little time to dwell on how the Leopard Lady had allied herself with the terrible group. He was fully occupied in keeping on her weaving trail that defied every traffic ordinance. Suddenly, quite as if by accident, the cream-colored car swerved to avoid a car coming from the opposite direction. Its front wheel clipped the corner of the curb and the car bounded into an alley.

"X" followed, wheeling his car across the street and into the alley. Ahead of him, the cream-colored car had slowed down. "X" spurted, and in another moment was forced to cram on his brakes with all the strength of his right leg. From a covered driveway, a huge truck had backed across the alley. The Agent was as effectually separated from his quarry as if a stone wall had suddenly been conjured up in front of him. In spite of his quick action and the superior power of his brakes he did not stop until the nose of his car had mashed against the panel of the truck.

Was this opportune intervention a coincidence? The Secret Agent thought not. Everything had fallen in too perfectly with the Leopard Lady's plan of escape. He could almost hear her husky, purring laugh of triumph.

"X" knocked open the door of his car and leaped to the pavement. In a moment his question was definitely answered. It was no coincidence; it was a perfectly laid trap set to catch one man — Secret Agent "X."

From the doorway of flanking buildings poured a small army of men — corpse-faced criminals from out of the past. With the confidence their numbers gave them, they rushed upon "X," blunt-nose automatics firmly gripped in their fists. The Agent drew his gun with his right hand, at the same time sending a short, jolting left to the side of the foremost criminal's head. The man dropped without a groan. "X's" gas gun, that marvelous weapon of his own development, hissed like a snake. A cloud of the powerful anesthetizing vapor blasted a second criminal into oblivion.

Completely surrounded, "X" fought like one possessed of the devil. He hacked at heads with the barrel of his gun, wary of using the gas with which it was loaded lest in the mad, battling maelstrom of humanity some of the anesthetizing fumes reach his own lungs. The gang, he knew, would avoid using their automatics lest the sound of shots draw in police interference.

"X" got a grip around the waist of one of his opponents, lifted the man bodily, and would have hurled him to the pavement had he not at that moment been struck a powerful blow from behind. Off balance, he sprawled to the pavement. Like starved wolves, the mob was upon him, holding him down by sheer weight of numbers. A gun barrel crashed into his head — once — twice. Agent "X" dipped into oblivion.

# III
## TORTURE

SECRET AGENT "X's" first sensation was that of motion. The cold air of speed was biting into his cheeks. He opened his eyes, and stared straight ahead of him where automobile headlamps were beaming down a dark and narrow street. He tried to move. He could only turn his head; his feet were lashed to the brake and clutch pedals of the speeding car, and his hands were firmly fastened to the steering wheel.

He could not speak. A hard, conical-shaped gag, similar to the old French *poire d'angoise* had forced his jaws apart. He looked about him. Dirty brick dwellings rushed by on either side of the street. The speedometer hovered around fifty, but aside from the helpless Secret Agent, the roadster was empty.

"X" tried to depress the brake pedal. It was fixed in place. It was impossible for him to turn the steering wheel or cut the gas. The motor rolled smoothly, guided by some gigantic, invisible force. Secret Agent "X," champion of justice, was riding, apparently driving, the mystery car which the corpse-criminals had made the terror of the city.

That the car was robot-driven seemed to be the only explanation. Looking back over his shoulder, "X" could see another car a block or more behind. It was possible, he knew, to steer a car by robot radio control from another car. Still, with a block or more distance between the two cars, it seemed impossible that the car in which "X" was riding could be so unerringly managed.

His first thought was that the mystery car in which he rode would be driven into some accident that would be fatal for "X." But surely a gang which killed as the corpse-criminal mob did, would not go to the trouble of trying to make one murder out of scores appear as an accident.

The mystery car suddenly slowed down as though unseen giants were hauling on the wheels. It turned the corner, rolled on to a choppy pavement, turned into a drive, and slid through dark garage doors. Instantly, the doors closed, and "X" was in a darkness like black velvet.

A moment of silence was followed by a strange, clanking sound. "X" was conscious of some one close at hand moving through the darkness. Something rattled on the door of the car. A cold claw of iron clutched about his left wrist and locked there. "X" struggled with all his Herculean strength to break his bonds. But they resisted his every effort. The clanging sound continued. Some one was rounding the nose of the car. Again a claw of steel met his flesh. A second bracelet of metal encircled his right wrist.

Then the beam of a flashlight struck down through the darkness, illuminating the under-cowl of the car. He heard the sound of heavy breathing. And in the reflected rays of light, Agent "X" saw the distorted features of Scar Fassler. A long knife was in the big mobster's hand. Its keen blade sliced through the cords that bound "X" to the pedals and steering wheel.

The Agent saw that his wrists were linked by a heavy log chain. A leader of steel cable ran from the chain to a loop set in the garage wall. Fassler grinned up into the Agent's face.

"Whyn't you try a sock at me now, Mr. 'X'," he goaded. "Which freshes up my memory to the fact that I owe you a poke, don't I?" Fassler's great fist fanned the air in a haymaker which "X" attempted to duck. But the blow landed on his jaw, sending flames of pain through his head, and setting his ears to ringing. The Agent gritted his teeth. Great muscles in his arms rippled and drew taut beneath his flesh. His steely eyes burned with cold fire.

Fassler grinned. "You goin' to get out, or do I knock you out?" He raised his right hand, balled around an automatic.

"X" shrugged, kicked open the door of the car, and stepped out. In spite of the weight of the chains, he carried himself perfectly erect. He moved easily across the garage toward the loop which confined him. Fassler followed.

When within a yard of the wall, Agent "X" turned around. With a speed that took Fassler completely unawares, "X" swung the heavy chain above his head, and brought it down in a blow that landed on Fassler's right forearm. A harsh cry of pain ripped from Fassler's throat. The automatic in his hand fell to the floor. "X" dropped to his knees and, manacled though he was, recovered the weapon.

The blow which he had given Fassler might easily have broken his arm. The gunman had dropped to the floor.

Suddenly, "X" heard a faint rustle behind him. He pivoted. A shadowy thing of uncertain shape swirled down upon him. His head was blanketed in a soft black rope that reeked with the sweetish odor of chloroform. To battle in such intoxicating darkness was hopeless. "X" felt himself seized in powerful arms. Then he became a floating thing without substance.

When Agent "X" came out of his drugged sleep, he found himself alone in a small room. A single door with a small barred window was the only break in the monotony of the four walls. He was dizzy and nauseated from the effects of the chloroform. For a few moments, he lay perfectly still upon the floor, eyes wandering about the room. Not far from him was a complex apparatus partially hidden by a black screen centered with an opaque window of some white material. This he recognized as the most up-to-date television receiver on the market.

For a while, he watched it dully, wondering what its purpose could be. Then he sat up. The manacles had been removed. He ran his fingers over his face to make sure that his makeup was intact.

At the instant that his fingers touched his face, his heart pounded in his throat. His groping fingers had not encountered plastic makeup material and faceplates, but his own face! He stared down at his fingers. Finger tips were stained with black ink. His disguise had been penetrated, and, for the first time in his dual career of crime fighting and law evasion, his fingerprints had been recorded. For the first time, the hideous phantom of failure danced mocking before his eyes. He had at last met his equal — the hidden leader of the corpse-legion whose butchery terrorized the city.

The one light in the room faded out, and was supplanted by the glow of the television screen. A powerful radio sound circuit moved into operation. Across the television screen, a black shadow moved. It was a shapeless shadow that might well have concealed a man. "X" watched it closely.

"We meet, Secret Agent 'X'," a voice boomed from the radio. "Rest assured that though my curiosity has led me to look upon your true face, no other eyes than mine have seen you as you really are. You would have been a worthy opponent hadn't the green eyes of the Leopard Lady enticed you into my trap. I have no particular desire to reveal your identity to the world unless it becomes necessary to do so.

"My plan, I think, will interest you. You may have guessed of the hate I bear all who support the law. And inasmuch as you are the paragon of law enforcement, my hatred has centered upon you. I have conceived a delightful means of tormenting you before you die — a means which is related to some extent to what those ancient monks of the Spanish Inquisition called 'Torture by Hope.' Observe the screen of the television unit carefully, Agent 'X', and you will understand perfectly."

The shadow was gone. Again a switch popped. Shadow objects on the television screen were brought into focus. Agent "X" saw an interior view of a house that was well known to him. It was the exotically furnished home of Felice Vincart, the Leopard Lady. Between two twisted pillars that might have been brought from Granada's Alhambra was an iron-barred cage containing two tawny leopards of unusual size.

The door of the cage was in the form of a circle of metal. It appeared that the door was made of many pieces of metal mounted and movable like the iris of a camera. A long pendulumed clock was mounted above it.

Agent "X" remembered that some strange whim of Felice Vincart had led her to install an amateur television transmitter in her home. Now he understood that it was to be put to a terrible purpose. On a gilt divan, directly in front of the leopard cage, was the form of a woman. In spite of the small proportions reproduced on the screen, "X" knew that woman. There was no mistaking the wealth of golden hair that rippled across the cushions of the divan. The woman was Betty Dale.

The Agent's heart throbbed in hopeless rebellion against what he feared he would be forced to witness. The helpless girl writhed against her bonds. Shudders convulsed her entire body as one of the leopards flung its tawny strength against the circular door. Then "X" knew the meaning of torture!

The great clock above the cage had been set in motion. Its long pendulum ticked out an eternity of minutes; and as each minute ticked by, the steel, irislike door opened the merest fraction of an inch. Eventually, that door would widen to such an extent that the big cats would break through. Their lean flanks, their gaping, hungry jaws gave mute promise of what might be expected.

Agent "X" sprang to his feet. The house was silent. There was no sign of any living thing within the room save the torturous, silent pantomime of the television screen. "X" leaped to the door. It was heavy oak three inches thick. "X" looked through the opening, looked anywhere save at the baleful picture on the screen.

In the hall outside, a powerfully built man lolled in a chair. A Winchester rifle was slung across his knees. The Agent's fingers trembled over the lock of the door. He might easily pick it if his tools had been left him.

He made a hasty inventory of the equipment he carried. His gas pistol had been removed from his coat as well as the automatic he had taken from Fassler. But his pocket makeup kit and compact tool and medical kits had been left him. "Why?" his brain hammered. Surely the shadowy gang leader was more clever than that. Did the Unknown imagine that Agent "X" could be confined in such a cell by even a dozen guards when the person whom he regarded above everyone else was in danger? Some sixth sense told him that here was a trick of some sort.

"X" snapped open his makeup kit and removed a small, cylindrical bottle. Inside of it were two crystal glass capsules filled with a colorless fluid. From the pocket of his vest, he pulled out what appeared to be an ordinary fountain pen. Removing the cap revealed that it was a hollow barrel. "X" took one of the capsules from the cylindrical bottle and dropped it into the fountain pen. He inserted one end of the pen between his lips. The pen had resolved itself into a conveniently small blow gun. He drew deep lungs full of air, sighted the tube on the lolling figure of the guard, and blew with all his strength.

The tiny glass capsule pinged against the wall a few inches above the guard's head, releasing a tiny cloud of fog. The guard sprang upright. The startled expression on his face was supplanted by one of inane peacefulness. He collapsed on the floor.[4]

The Agent thrust the blowgun back into his pocket, and immediately went to work on the lock. Tiny, finely tempered tools, the product of a professional lockpick, dropped from the Agent's tool kit. In spite of the panic which possessed him, "X's" hands were perfectly steady as he guided a gleaming tool into the tumblers of the lock. There had not been sufficient quantity of his anesthetizing gas in the tiny capsule to keep the guard unconscious for long. Eagerness, triumph, and doubt were expressions that alternately crossed the Agent's almost boyish features.

In another moment, the lock was released. A backward glance at the television screen showed him that the circular door in the leopard cage had opened far enough to permit one of the savage beasts to thrust its drooling muzzle through the opening.

Agent "X" sprang into the hall. Without looking to right or left, he made for the door beside which the guard had lolled. A simple skeleton lock yielded to the key which "X" extracted from the guard's pocket. Then he plunged down the stairs, and into the dismal street.

He was several miles from the house of the exotic Leopard Lady, and in such a district, at such a late hour, there wasn't a taxi in sight. However, parked a short distance from the house from which he had escaped, was a

---

[4] AUTHOR'S NOTE: In the constant war Agent "X" wages against crime, he is forced to employ new tricks as often as possible so that his movements are seldom anticipated by his enemies. He is constantly on the lookout for new devices to strengthen his defense. This simple pocket blow gun, with its special missiles containing a form of his anesthetizing vapor, is one of the products of his own inventive genius.

car. He ran to it, opened the door, and turned his flashlight on the instrument panel. The key was in the ignition lock.

Again that strange premonition that this was not a coincidence passed over Agent "X." It was all too easy—his escape and the finding of a car that must enable him to reach the Leopard Lady's house in time. But this was not a time for hesitation. He was certain of trickery somewhere, but the scene he had witnessed on the screen of the television set could not have been faked.

IN a moment, he was speeding down the street, steering with one hand and fumbling with the makeup kit which he had opened on the seat beside him. He needed no light for the disguise he was about to assume.[5]

Thick layers of plastic volatile material lent a heaviness to his face. Dark pigments rubbed into his jowls simulated blue-black beard stubble. Plastic material widened his nose. The dark toupee which he had used in the character of Peter Krausman had not been removed by the gang chief. By the time the car nosed into a suburban residential district, he appeared to be an entirely different person than the man who had left the dismal back street fifteen minutes before.

The house that Felice Vincart had inherited from her wealthy husband was one of somber gray stone approached by a winding drive of white gravel. Agent "X" parked the car in front of the gate, got out and crossed the

---

[5] AUTHOR'S NOTE: The genius of Agent "X" in the matter of disguise and voice impersonation is well known to the regular reader of these records. Because he never knows when he will be called upon to effect a complete change of features in a few moments' time, he has practiced certain stock disguises until he knows them well enough to permit him to assume them without the aid of a mirror and in the dark if need be.

drive to the velvety lawn. There he broke into a run, eyes strained ahead to catch some sign of life in the great house. If there were lights inside, every curtain had been securely drawn.

"X" sprang up the steps of the portico. The door was locked, but it required him only a moment to unlock it with the aid of his special master keys. He entered the hall, needling the darkness with his flashlight. Everywhere were furnishings that reflected the exotic personality of the woman who owned the house. "X" pushed back a door of carved wood and crossed a sumptuous living room. He stopped stock still, listening for the moment to the sound of bestial claws rasping over some metal surface. He sprang to a great oak-paneled door and flung it wide.

The pale light from a pierced brass lamp reflected upon a high, carved ceiling, and the narrow twisted pillars of the Leopard Lady's drawing room. In a gloomy corner of the room, he saw two pairs of baleful yellow eyes. "X" rounded the bulky apparatus of the television transmitting equipment. He inhaled sharply. Crouching near the golden divan to which Betty Dale was bound, was the lithe form of a huge leopard. Aside from the switching tip of its tail, it was entirely motionless.

"X" sprang toward the big cat. He swept up a chair. The beast turned, and launched itself straight for him. The chair in the Agent's hands swung up above his head, meeting the hurtling yellow shadow in the midsection. But the weight of the animal sent "X" crashing to the floor. With a snarl, the beast's forepaws lashed out. Powerful claws ripped splinters of wood from the chair.

Every muscle in the Agent's powerful body was brought into play in a mighty heave that hurled the leopard to one side. "X" sprang to his feet. His eyes darted toward the cage. The second leopard crouched in the circular door of the enclosure. "X's" lips puckered. He uttered a piercing whistle. The effect of that whistle on the beasts was remarkable. The muscles of the leopard in the cage relaxed. The other beast slunk into a corner, and sat down upon its haunches.[6]

Agent "X" sprang to the couch to which Betty Dale was tied. Apparently, she was unharmed, though unconscious. The agony of waiting for that circular door to open and free the hungry beasts had been too much for her. She had fainted. "X" took out his pocket knife and cut the cords that bound her. He was in the act of taking his medical kit from his pocket in order to give Betty suitable stimulant, when a soft, husky laugh sounded behind him. "X" pivoted.

Felice Vincart stood not ten feet away. A dark traveling suit hugged her slender form. Her peculiar greenish eyes were smoky behind the wisp of veil on her smart hat. Her slender, gloved hand held a small automatic.

"I advise you," she said softly, "to put up your hands. I am rather a good shot. I would not hesitate to shoot an ordinary house breaker."

Agent "X" regarded the woman calmly. He closed his medical kit, and returned it to his pocket, but not until he had craftily palmed a small glass capsule in his right hand.

"Put up your hands." The woman's purring voice was unaltered. Slowly, "X" raised his hands above his head.

"I suppose you know who I am?" he asked.

The Leopard Lady shrugged. "I am sure I have no way of knowing. I've been a little out of touch with the

---

[6] AUTHORS NOTE: One of the mysteries revolving about Secret Agent "X" is his peculiar influence over animals. This weird whistle which he utters upon occasion seems to have a fascination for all beasts who hear it. The magnetism of his glance probably also plays a part in this strange power he has over animals.

East, having just returned from California half an hour ago."

"X" was certain that she was laughing at him. He leaned slightly forward, throwing his weight on the balls of his feet. The woman turned her head slightly and uttered a sharp command in French. "X" saw the leopard get up from its corner and slink toward the cage. In another moment it was inside the cage beside its mate.

The Leopard Lady moved toward the couch where Betty Dale lay. "One of your victims, or a partner in crime?" she asked softly. She brought her left wrist up ever so slightly. For a moment, her eyes rested upon her watch. It was a movement that another man might have missed or misinterpreted. But Agent "X" knew that the Leopard Lady was expecting some one to come to her assistance. It was, as he had expected, some sort of a trap into which he had been forced to walk.

But action was imperative. His legs shot out like two springs, hurling him toward the woman. She fired instantly, the bullet jerking at the Agent's coat sleeve. "X's" left hand chopped down to lock over the woman's gun wrist. With a quick, twisting motion that brought a wince of pain from Felice Vincart, "X" disarmed her. But hardly had he obtained the gun before the doors at the opposite ends of the room opened.

"Reach for the ceiling!" a voice well known to "X" bellowed. He dropped the gun, raised his hands, and turned, slowly. Through the door at the rear of the room, came Inspector John Burks followed by six policemen. "X" looked over his shoulder at the other door, weighing his chance of escape. But at the other door stood Commissioner Foster, and his jumpy little friend, Major Derrick. Behind them was a second group of policemen.

# IV

## FRAMED

THE red lips of the Leopard Lady curved into a brilliant smile. "Thank you very much, Commissioner Foster. I was afraid, right after I called you, that this man would leave before you could capture him. I decided to risk holding him until you came."

"A nice piece of work, Miss Vincart," commended Foster. "Burks, search that man. If that tip was on the straight, he's a member of that gang the papers call the Corpse Legion."

"Why, what do you mean?" demanded the Leopard Lady.

It was Major Derrick's whipping voice that answered her question. "Just before you called, Commissioner Foster had a tip that your house was being used as a headquarters for the Corpse Legion while you were in California. It isn't the first time that criminals have made use of empty houses."

The Leopard Lady bit her lip. A worried frown crossed her face. "You don't think that I will be involved in any way in this business, do you?" she asked appealingly.

"Don't worry, lady, you've done your part in capturing this bird. We won't bother you any longer than is absolutely necessary," said Inspector Burks. He stepped through the ring of detectives around Secret Agent "X." He regarded the Agent a moment through half closed eyes. "Well, sir, either you're Secret Agent 'X' or some member of his gang!"

He glanced up at "X's" raised right hand; it was tightly closed over the glass capsule he had taken from the medical kit when the Leopard Lady had put in her appearance. "Open up that hand, you," ordered Burks.

A slow smile crossed "X's" features. "How do you know, if I am Secret Agent 'X' as you suppose, that my hand does not contain sure death for you?"

"I'll take that chance," said Burks gruffly. "You're pretty fond of your own skin."

"X" opened his right hand. It was empty. It had required but the tiniest gesture for him to drop the little glass capsule into the sleeve of his upraised arm. It would be instantly available whenever he wanted it.

Inspector Burks grunted his disappointment, and proceeded to search each one of the Agent's pockets. In the meantime Foster, Major Derrick, and the Leopard Lady were busy over Betty Dale.

"She's just fainted, poor girl," declared Foster. "Look at her wrists. She's been tied. Looks as though the gang had gone in for kidnapping as well as robbery. I am afraid, Miss Vincart, that your leopards are not as good watch dogs as you imagined them to be."

"Ah, no, my leopards are as pet kittens. They would hurt no one. But are you sure this girl is not associated with your strange criminal gang?" asked the Leopard Lady.

"Why, this is Betty Dale, a reporter on one of the local papers," explained Foster. "Her father was on the police force back in Major Derrick's day — eh, Derrick?"

"Of course, of course," jerked Derrick. "Miss Vincart, if you have a little brandy in the house, I think we can revive this young lady in a moment. She will probably be able to tell us enough about our prisoner to put him behind bars for the rest of his life."

"Certainly. A cellarette over there—"

Major Derrick started for the cellarette the Leopard Lady had indicated. In doing so, he tripped over something which extended out from beneath the edge of the couch on which Betty lay.

Inspector Burks quickly went over, demanded — "What the devil have we here?" He saw that Derrick had tripped over the end of a small black traveling bag that had seen considerable wear.

"This anything of yours?" asked Derrick of the Leopard Lady.

Felice Vincart's lips curved into a slight sneer. "Dear me, no. All of my traveling gear is upstairs waiting for the maid to unpack."

Burks, Derrick, and Foster knelt beside the black bag and opened the clasps. The opening of the bag was too much of a surprise for even Commissioner Foster to retain his usual composure. "Good Lord!" he gasped. "It's filled with jewels!"

"And —" Derrick said excitedly, "I recognize some of the pieces. There's the necklace stolen by the corpse-gang from Mr. Nelson's store. There's not another like it in the world!"

Inspector Burks looked over at Agent "X." He nodded his great head up and down slowly. "We've made a catch this time!"

A commotion arose at the opposite end of the room. A uniformed messenger was allowed to pass the police guarding the door. "Message for Commissioner Foster," the youth announced, extending a plain white envelope to the commissioner.

"Where from?" demanded Foster as he tore at the envelope.

The messenger shrugged. "Don't know. A man gave it to me at the telegraph office. He said it was for you. I've hunted for you for some time; then some one told me at headquarters that I might find you here."

Though Foster had asked the question, it is doubtful if he listened to the explanation, so intent was he upon the contents of the envelope. "Listen to this, Derrick," he said, his voice trembling slightly with excitement: " 'You have a friend in the enemy camp, Commissioner. I am enclosing the fingerprints of Secret Agent 'X'. Advise you checking them with any members of the gang you may capture.' "

Foster held up the slip of paper which had been enclosed with the message. Even from where he stood, Agent "X" could make out a complete set of fingerprints recorded on the paper. His heart gave a leap into his throat. The secret he had sworn would die with him — the secret of his identity — was about to be revealed. Even if he should succeed in escaping, the police now had a permanent record which could send him to the electric chair any time they laid their hands on him.[7]

But when another man might have spent precious moments brooding upon his own doom, Secret Agent "X" went into action. The hand of his upraised left arm balled and drove down like a mallet in a brain-rocking blow to the head of the plainclothes man in front of him. It was a blow that might have felled an ox. The Secret Agent hurdled the sprawled form, and ran straight at Foster. He knew that no one would dare fire a shot for fear of hitting the commissioner.

So sudden were his movements that surprise paralyzed everyone for a moment. "X," with head lowered, drove straight between Foster and Major Derrick. His

---

[7] AUTHOR'S NOTE: The Agent's unorthodox methods have been grossly misinterpreted by the members of the police force. They believe him to be a dangerous criminal. On several occasions, crimes with which "X" has had no connection have been laid at his door. The casebook of Inspector Burks is filled with records of crimes attributed to Agent "X". It is Burks' belief that Agent "X" will stop at nothing — even murder — to gain his own ends.

hand shot out. His fingers ripped the fingerprint record from Foster's hand. It was a single motion in his mad dash toward the door at the rear of the room.

Ahead of him, police guards massed before the door.

"Stop him!" shouted Burks. "Stop Agent 'X'!"

But even as Burks shouted, "X's" right arm dropped and rose again. That motion had sent the little glass capsule he had secreted down into the palm of his hand. As he ran, he threw it with all his strength at the group of police massed against the door. At the same instant, he drew a deep breath and dived into the center of the police in the doorway. They fell like cardboard soldiers before his furious onslaught. The glass capsule he had broken in their midst contained sufficient anesthetizing gas to send them all into temporary oblivion.

"X" TORE away from enfeebled hands, hurdled recumbent bodies that cluttered the floor, broke through the door, closed and locked it behind him. As heavy shoulders battered at the locked door, threatening to burst its hinges, Agent "X" sprang up the flight of broad stairs that extended before him. At the top of the stairs, he turned into the first room he came to. It was a large bathroom. He leaped to the window. But a glance out the window showed him that it offered no avenue of escape. It would have been a twenty foot drop, and already the shadowy forms of the police were moving across the lawn, surrounding the house.

"X" could hear the sound of feet hurrying up the stairs. Without any arms other than his wits and his fists, he would probably be completely at their mercy. He turned around, opened a small door which he supposed to be a closet of some sort. His heart gave a bound; for the door opened on the dark, narrow shaft of a laundry chute.

Without a moment's hesitation, he threw a leg over

the frame of the small door, arched his back so as to wedge himself in place, and pulled the door shut behind him. Thrusting his elbows against the walls of the chute in order to break the speed of his descent, he began sliding down the chute.

A second later, he had dropped into a laundry room in the basement. Only a little gray light passed through the basement windows, but after the tomblike darkness of the clothes chute, this light was sufficient for him to see his way about. He went from the laundry into the furnace room in search of a way out.

In the heels of his shoes were secret compartments where he carried materials which had often aided him in getting out of tight spots. He would probably have to employ the tube of makeup material which one of his heels contained, in order to effect a disguise that would enable him to get out of the house.

But his first task was to destroy the record of his fingerprints which he had snatched from Foster. Light from a basement window pointed out a monstrous furnace which heated the house. It was far too late in the spring for him to hope that there would be a fire inside the furnace. But near at hand, he found a small glass containing matches. He opened the glass jar, took out a match, and scuffed it against the floor.

It was only after he had crushed the charred scrap of paper beneath his heel that his old self-confidence returned to him. Now, with a little good fortune, the great work which he had undertaken could go on.

As he turned from the little pile of black paper ash which had once marked him for certain doom, he bumped directly against the muzzle of an automatic pistol. The brilliant beam of a flashlight burned into his eyes, blinding him.

"Got you this time, Secret Agent 'X'."

Instantly, "X" recognized that voice. It was the voice

of one of Burks' best men, Detective Keegan.[8]

"And I'm not taking any chances, either!" The detective's flashlight described a brilliant arc above the Agent's head and descended in a blow to "X's" temple. Agent "X" dropped to the basement floor, and lay still.

A few minutes later, Detective Keegan, hat mashed down over his head, triumphantly entered the presence of Inspector John Burks who was bellowing orders to his men. Betty Dale, in the meantime, had recovered under the apparently kindly ministrations of Felice Vincart.

"Find anything in the basement, Keegan?" demanded Burks.

Keegan coolly nodded as he shook a cigarette from a battered pack. "Secret Agent 'X'," he replied between puffs of smoke.

"Agent 'X'!" Burks sprang across the room, and clamped both hands down on Keegan's shoulders. "You found him, and let him slip through your fingers without giving us a signal? By heaven, you'll lose your badge for this!"

Keegan spread his right hand, palm down. "Easy, sir. I've got your Agent 'X' all tied up with sash cord. I brained him with my flash. He'll keep for weeks."

Had Burks been watching Betty Dale, he would have seen her cheeks grow deathly pale.

Burks' eyes seemed to pop from their sockets. "Foster!" he cried. "We — we've — he's got Secret Agent 'X'!" Burks thundered through the room and out into the kitchen. He plunged down the basement steps, closely

---

[8] AUTHOR'S NOTE: It will be remembered that Agent "X" met Keegan in his long battle against a master extortionist who threatened his victims with an insidious chemical weapon known as "The Amber Death." The instance of this meeting was recorded in the novel entitled "The Golden Ghoul."

followed by Foster, Major Derrick, and several men of the force.

In the furnace room, Burks knelt before a recumbent figure. The man was securely tied with a soot-soiled rope. Burks turned him over. It was indeed the heavy-faced man whom Burks had declared to be Secret Agent "X."

"So that's the devil!" exclaimed Derrick. "Got him at last. No more police massacres, Foster. This man ought to be lynched!"

Burks was staring down into the face of the unconscious man. "You got to hand it to him," he muttered. "You wouldn't know that face he's wearing from real flesh and blood! But there's a way of finding out what's underneath."

The inspector dug his fingernails deep into the plastic material that enabled "X" to adopt any feature he chose. His hands trembled with suppressed excitement. Time after time, this mystery man had defeated Burks. He could scarcely believe that at last he was about to look upon the true features of his old enemy.

"Keegan shall have a promotion for this!" declared Foster.

Burks said enthusiastically: "Keegan's good, but I don't see —" His sentence wandered off into a whisper. His hands dropped limply to his sides. Foster and Derrick looked at each other and then down at Burks. Words failed the inspector. Unconsciously, he molded bits of plastic makeup material between his fingers, and stared down at the face of the man on the floor. For the man who had been so completely knocked out, the man who had been so securely tied, was none other than Detective Keegan himself.

# V

## *THE DUMMY*

THE actions of Secret Agent "X" from the moment that Keegan had swung his flashlight in an effort to knock him out, were as simple as they were surprising. Keegan was a powerful man, and perfectly fit. But he had acted hastily. In almost complete darkness, it is difficult to strike a man in a vulnerable spot at the first blow. The detective's flashlight, aimed at the Agent's temple, had grazed "X's" ear and landed squarely on his right shoulder.

"X" had collapsed on the floor to lie perfectly still. The moment that Keegan had pocketed his gun and started to kneel at his captive's side, "X" had thrown up both legs to lock in a powerful scissors grip around Keegan's knees. The detective had fallen full length upon "X" and had taken a short, chopping left on the head.

The struggle had not lasted a minute. Keegan was no match for the fighting skill of Agent "X." Having tied the detective and appropriated his flashlight, "X" proceeded to remove makeup material from his own face. Then, using makeup material which he obtained from one of the secret compartments in his heel, "X" worked over his own face to resemble the contours of Keegan's face. Master of his art that he was, "X" was able to duplicate Keegan's features from memory. A change of clothing, and he was ready to face Inspector Burks.

No sooner had Burks and his followers trooped into the basement, than Agent "X" sauntered out of the house, and regained the car he had borrowed.

The sky was graying in the east by the time "X"

arrived at one of his hideouts miles away from the Leopard Lady's house. He knew that Betty Dale was in good hands. Burks, who had known the girl since childhood, would not have permitted any harm to come to her. But "X" knew that more than ever before, the police would hamper his efforts in the cause of justice.

The Agent's first act on reaching his hideout — a brownstone dwelling in the west end of town — was to enter a closet and open what appeared to be a large wardrobe trunk. Inside was concealed a small shortwave radio transmitter and receiver. By means of a telegraph key, he tapped out a code message which was transmitted on a clear wave channel. He was anxious to get in touch with Harvey Bates, director of the Agent's vast secret organization.[9]

Almost immediately, the reply came through — a series of Morse dots and dashes. Again, the Agent's key clicked, this time to inform Bates to use a certain code, known only to Bates and himself. Then he tapped out a question which when decoded read: "Are camera planes ready for immediate use?"

Bates replied that two of the Agent's aerial eyes were ready to take off at a moment's notice.

"Then," the Agent tapped out, "put them in the air at once. Patrol city. Watch for Corpse-Legion's mystery car.

---

9  AUTHOR'S NOTE: Considerably larger than the Hobart Agency is the group of men and women selected by "X" to comprise his staff of intelligence workers, and directed by Harvey Bates. Unlike the Hobart group, the world does not know of the existence of the Bates organization. Bates recognizes his chief only by a certain voice the Agent uses when communicating by telephone or radiophone, or by one of the codes which he employs in telegraphic transmission. Both of the organizations are paid for their services from an almost inexhaustible fund contributed for the Agent's use by certain public-spirited men.

## 52  LEGION OF THE LIVING DEAD

In case of another police massacre, trace car, and deliver record of route taken."[10]

Having completed these instructions, "X" leisurely removed his makeup which had aided him in the impersonation of Detective Keegan. Seated before a triple mirror, his skillful fingers worked miracles. Transparent adhesive twisted his lips into an ugly snarl. Plastic material helped him achieve a hideous, flattened nose that was almost apelike. A clever toupee of coarse, black hair, a suit of flagrant checks, and a tie that flamed completed his disguise.

Staring for a moment at his reflection in the mirror, he believed that his new face was the result of genuine inspiration. He looked the sort of a man a policeman would arrest on sight. He could think of no face which appeared to need the aid of a plastic surgeon any more than the one reflected in the mirror.

It was his intention to visit the home and office of Jules Planchard. Previous investigation had led "X" to believe that the greedy doctor was not above using his skill to change the features of fugitives from justice. So far, Planchard had slipped beneath the fingers of the law; but "X's" great group of secret investigators had ferreted out Planchard's true character. Then the incident of the jade bracelet — first purchased by Planchard and next

---

[10] AUTHOR'S NOTE: It will be remembered the Agent "X" used this aerial device first in that adventure which was recorded in the novel entitled, "The Murder Monster." It consists of an automatic moving picture camera mounted beneath the cockpit of an airplane. This camera is controlled by the pilot of the ship. What he sees through a glassed-in opening in the floor of the plane, is recorded on the film of the camera. This device is one of the Agent's most valuable accessories inasmuch as once sighted by the pilot of the plane, the camera produces a permanent record of the action of the crime, and the route taken by the escaping criminals.

seen on the wrist of Felice Vincart — made "X" doubly suspicious.

"X" believed that there were but two possible explanations for the existence of the Corpse-Legion. Either some scientist had discovered a means of reviving the dead, or there was trickery somewhere — trickery of a sort that "X" knew better than any other man. Such trickery — the alteration of the real features of a man's face — could be greatly simplified if the skilled Jules Planchard served the unknown leader of the gang.

It was nine o'clock in the morning when "X," beneath his masterly disguise, pressed the doorbell of Jules Planchard's great square, brick house. His ring was answered by a servant whose eyes were still puffy with sleep. Dr. Planchard, the servant informed "X," was still at breakfast.

"Don't let that bother you, buddy," the Agent growled. He wedged the toe of his left shoe in between door and sill. "The doc's expectin' me. I'm a customer, get it?" He winked knowingly.

The servant would have hesitated to admit "X" had not the latter suddenly thrown his full weight against the door. The servant fell backwards. "X" strode into the hall, slamming and locking the door behind him.

The servant cowered against the wall, staring at the leather-covered blackjack that "X" swung suggestively.

"You lead me to the doc, old wooden face, 'fore I bash your brains out!" Agent "X" snarled.

"He — he didn't want to see anybody. He's —"

"Ah, Parkins, what seems to be the trouble?" a nasal voice inquired.

"X" turned. Dr. Jules Planchard, swathed in a quilted silk dressing gown, stood in the door at the end of the hall. His long goatee dangled beneath his pendulous lower lip. He examined "X" with keen, black-bean eyes. His breakfast napkin was in his right hand.

"This bird thought he was keeping' me out, doc," replied "X" familiarly. He thrust thumbs into the arm holes of his checkered vest, tilted his hat on the back of his head, and glowered at the doctor. "My name's Vance, 'Dummy' Vance. Maybe me name hasn't got this far east, but out in Frisco I'm called 'Dummy' — cause that's the one thing I'm not. You look like a smart man yourself, doc."

Planchard bowed slightly in acknowledgment of what was intended to be a compliment.

"Smart enough," the Agent continued, "not to kick up too much fuss when a guy wants his map dredged a bit. This beezer, now —" the Agent fingered his flattened nose — "without that, the bulls wouldn't know me from a wooden Indian. You gettin' the idea?"

Planchard motioned to the door through which he had just passed. "Come in here, Mr. Vance. We can talk in privacy."

"X" followed Planchard through the door into a small study. Planchard motioned to a chair across from a small coffee table laden with the doctor's breakfast. "X" dropped into a chair, picked up a couple of slices of toast, and munched thoughtfully for a moment. His eyes narrowed.

"That gun you're hidin' under your napkin, doc — I spotted it first time I lamped you. Kind of spoils my digestion to have to eat starin' at a gun."

Planchard coughed nervously, dropped his napkin, and put a small automatic into his pocket. "One never knows," he mumbled.

"Sure. And that's why you got to fix me up so I look like a Sunday-school teacher. I worked myself over from the west coast, if you get what I mean. Maybe I left a record here and there, and maybe I didn't. How'd you like to earn a grand fixin' my pan?"

Planchard smiled slightly. "Really, Mr. Vance, you and I don't speak the same language!"

"X" scowled. "You mean you come higher than that?"

Planchard nodded. "For a man of your reputation, I don't think five thousand would be too much to ask."

"X" tossed a crumb of toast into his mouth and chewed it. "Okay, make it five grand. But it's got to be a swell job."

"Just step into my operating room," Planchard suggested, "and we'll see what can be done. Of course," he added, as he led toward the door, "I'll have to have part of my fee in advance."

"Fair enough," the Agent said, handing him a thousand dollars. He followed the doctor through a door, down a short hall, and into a small operating room that was complete in every detail. The doctor went over to a white-enameled locker where he traded dressing gown for a short white coat.

"X" removed his hat, and slung one leg over the white operating table. The doctor went over to the wall and switched on a powerful compound lamp suspended above the Agent's head. He walked to a cabinet, picked up a gleaming scalpel, and approached "X."

"Let's see —" Planchard tilted the Agent's head, and stared long and searchingly into his face. For a moment, "X" wondered if even his clever disguise could withstand such a scrutiny. He eyed the scalpel uneasily.

"Don't you give an anesthetic or nothin'?" he asked.

Planchard laughed. "Oh, I can't operate today. I'm merely studying the lines of your face. Your nose is really horrible, if you don't mind my saying so. I can make an incision here — " the scalpel tapped the bridge of the Agent's nose. "Possibly one here." Suddenly, Planchard brought his scalpel down beneath "X's" chin. Its gleaming point pressed against "X's" throat. "Now, blundering spy, tell me why you have come here!" Planchard whipped out. "One of your gang has tricked me already. What did you do with my formula?" His left arm swung around behind "X," and gripped his shoulders tightly. "Tell me, I say, or I operate right now — on your jugular!"

"Wh-what formuler?" the Agent stuttered. "Don't getcha."

"You know well enough! No man of your sort comes here without a letter of introduction from some one whom I can trust. You must be a spy. Tell me what you have done with my formula! Doubtless you have come to get further information about it. If that formula becomes public property, I shall be ruined. Tell me, or by heaven, I will kill you!"

Agent "X's" right leg kicked around behind Planchard, and stuck him behind the knees. At the same time, he sent a pounding blow to the doctor's midsection, and snatched at the hand that held the scalpel against his throat.

Planchard doubled beneath the force of the blow, staggered back, and tripped over the Agent's right leg. "X" sprang toward the doctor. He yanked his gas-gun from his pocket. Rage blinded the surgeon. He sprang up from the floor, and flung himself upon "X." His fingers wilted on the Agent's throat as he received a full charge from the gas gun straight in the face. "X" picked the man up, and stretched him out on his own operating table.

A soft, purring laugh sounded behind "X." He swung around. A revolver shot cracked out. The Leopard Lady stood in the door of the operating room, a smoking revolver in her hand. Both of the Agent's hands were clasped tightly over his heart. Thick, red fluid crawled from between his fingers. He staggered toward the Leopard Lady. His knees melted under him. He fell full length on the floor.

A cruel smile spread slowly across the face of the Leopard Lady. Then her green eyes darted at the operating table where Dr. Planchard lay. With quick, graceful steps, she crossed the room, and bent over the doctor. She held his wrist a moment, feeling his pulse. Then her red lips puckered and she uttered a sharp whistle.

From beneath veiled eyelids, Agent "X" watched what went on in the room. He had sustained no more painful injury than if he had been struck a hard blow over the heart with a man's fist. His bullet proof vest had stopped the Leopard Lady's shot. However, Secret Agent "X" often had occasion to "play possum." Beneath his clothing, he frequently wore a small bladder containing a quantity of red dye which closely resembled human blood.[11]

By pinching this bladder between his hands, he had opened a valve that allowed some of the substance to flow out between his fingers. Coupled with his natural dramatic talents, this trick enabled him to feign death without difficulty.

NO sooner had the Leopard Lady uttered her whistle than two men stepped into the room. Again, "X" met faces out of the past. One of the men had the face of Willy Hymes; and "X" had last seen Willy Hymes on a slab in the morgue. He had been killed in a gun brawl. Yet here, to all appearances, was Hymes in the flesh. More than ever, "X" was convinced that Planchard had played some part in this hideous hoax. Planchard had lost a formula. "X" had a notion as to the use that formula had been put, and also a vague idea as to the identity of the criminal genius behind the gang.

"We will take Dr. Planchard to the chief," declared

---

[11] AUTHOR'S NOTE: This dye which simulated blood, it will be remembered, was used by the Agent when he was engaged in conflict with the strange criminal society known as The Seven Silent Men. On that occasion, the dye was used when he was forced to pretend to murder Betty Dale. The incident was recorded in the story entitled, "The Corpse Cavalcade."

the Leopard Lady. "He is becoming annoying, and I believe he has begun to suspect me. Carry him to the car at once."

Without reply, rat-faced Willy Hymes and his equally despicable-looking companion lifted the doctor, and carried him from the room. The Leopard Lady saw them out, then crossed to where "X" lay. She gave him a sharp kick between the shoulders with her tiny, high-heeled slipper. Though that kick had struck a particularly sensitive nerve center, "X" did not move. The Leopard Lady laughed softly, and left the room.

"X" lay still, scarcely breathing until he heard the tap of her shoes far down the hall. Then he got up, crossed to the door. The Leopard Lady and her companions had left the house by means of the back door. "X" entered Planchard's office. On the floor was the surgeon's servant. There was a red lump at the back of the man's ear. Evidently, this was the work of the Leopard Lady's two bodyguards.

Having made sure that the servant would be unconscious for some time, "X" picked up the doctor's telephone and called a number which had never appeared in any telephone directory. Speaking into the transmitter, the harsh voice which had identified him as "Dummy" Vance slipped down into a smooth, deep pitch. It was the one voice by which Harvey Bates recognized his chief.

"Bates," ordered the Agent, "have the house of Felice Vincart watched. Try to shadow anyone who enters or leaves."

"Right, Chief," replied Bates. "Have two men in that district now. They can reach the Vincart house in a few minutes. Just a moment, please. Have further information."

The Agent waited until he again heard Bates' voice. He could hear the rustle of his henchman's report sheets.

"Sleepy Meguire," Bates announced, "former public enemy who was incarcerated in the state penitentiary, has been granted special parole. This information has not been made public. Our agents inform us that Meguire has been out of prison nearly a week. He convinced authorities that, given a month of freedom, he could lay hands on the man responsible for the police massacres. Meguire's brother is being held in prison as hostage.

"Half an hour ago, another robbery and police killing took place — the former at the Graystone National Bank and the latter three blocks west. Our own agents positively identified a man seen loitering near the bank a few minutes before the robbery as Meguire. He is living in the Armedale Apartments under the name of Randolph Schnell."

"Good!" the Agent rapped. "Anything more? Any information regarding Peter Krausman, the jeweler?"

"Krausman was seen to enter his own apartment early this morning," replied Bates. "All of our efforts to locate the gang's mystery car from the air were failures. Pilots report visibility poor."

"Keep trying," urged "X" cheerfully. He hung up the receiver.

# *VI*
## *KRAUSMAN'S SECRET*

HAD Mr. Randolph Schnell's neighbors in the Armedale Apartments known anything about Mr. Schnell beside the fact that he drove a Lincoln and paid four hundred dollars a month rent, they would have probably packed their belongings and vacated immediately. "Sleepy" Meguire, otherwise known as Randolph Schnell, did not look like an ex-convict. With his suits, shoes, ties, and socks all of the softest shades of brown, Mr. Schnell looked the gentleman — or at least a gentleman's gentleman.

He was in the act of distractedly accepting an invitation to bridge when the door of his apartment opened, and he was confronted with a surly-faced, tow-headed youth whose clothes were shiny and who obviously didn't care. Half an hour before, another makeup miracle had gone on before the triple mirror of Secret Agent "X." And when "X" had left his hideout he had stepped directly into the character of "Butch" Bently, former torpedo in Meguire's group of criminals.

Mr. Meguire registered alarm. The sudden appearance of this man placed Meguire in a precarious spot; for it was well known that Bently was scheduled to walk through Sing Sing's little green door, and be carried back.

Meguire dropped his French type telephone, sprang to his feet, and got behind his chair. "Get out of here!" he snarled.

The tow-headed young man with the mauler's face closed the door behind him, and walked over to replace the phone that Meguire had carelessly dropped.

"A dame pulled that on me once," explained Bently in a voice that was hardly more than a squeak. "All she and me had to say got out over the telephone wire. Wasn't long before I had to leave town and rest up."

"How — how'd you get out of stir?" asked Meguire huskily.

"Walked out," explained Agent "X" in the voice of "Butch" Bently. "Them screws is all dumb. And 'memberin' how you and me used to be pals, I thought I'd come here."

"What do you want? Money?"

Eagerly, the magnificent Meguire reached for his check book.

"Nope," the Agent declined. "Just some info. I know you didn't get paroled just to go to bridge parties. And havin' measured your streak of yellow, I know you're not out to get this guy called 'X' who's supposed to be runnin' this gang that's tearin' the town apart. You'd light out if you thought you might accidentally bump into him."

Meguire's heavy eyelids drooped. He licked fat lips that had suddenly gone dry. "Well, to tell you the truth, I had a little business I had to take care of. It was a little awkward in stir trying to transact business."

"X" nodded. "Now, let's have all the truth. What kind of hot stuff are you tryin' to handle now?"

"Just a few jewels, and a carload of silk we picked up before Christmas," explained Meguire. "I'm willing to give you your split. Remember —" as "X" came a step nearer — "I offered to split before you asked me."

"X" shook his head in mute negation. His eyes never left Meguire's perpetually tired face. Suddenly, Meguire's hand struck at his coat pocket. He drew an automatic. "You get out of here!" he growled.

"X" smiled. "Still packin' them — eh? Well, I'd as soon be plugged by you as be fried in the chair. I'd know you'd follow me straight to hell when they found out you did it. Besides, even with a slug in me, I could choke you just like this!"

"X" sprang like a cat. His long fingers were wide spread. Panic gripped Meguire. The gun fell from his nerveless fingers. "X" kicked it to one side. His arms dropped. The ugly mouth that he had adopted, sneered. "Still yellow. Now you speak up before I tear you apart!"

Meguire raked his perspiring face with a trembling hand. "You ask me anything. I'll tell you anything I know. But you gotta get out."

"Okay." The Agent scuffed a match on his thumb nail, and lighted a cigarette. "Who fences that stuff for you?"

"Peter Krausman," whispered Meguire; "but if you let on I told you, I'm done for!"

"I'd feel tough about that! So Krausman, the big-shot jeweler, is also a number one fence? And you wouldn't mind confirming the fact that Krausman is also working with this gang of cop butchers?"

Meguire turned the color of dough. "I — I didn't say that!" He seized "X's" coat lapels and hung there, his eyes pleading for the Agent's silence.

"When are you goin' to see Krausman?" the Agent persisted.

"In about fifteen minutes. He's coming here. I tried to meet him by appointment in front of a bank a while ago, but he didn't show up. But he's coming here now, and you've got to get out!"

"X" pulled on his cigarette and held it almost beneath Meguire's nose. In another moment, there was a faint pop. The cigarette in the Agent's fingers disintegrated. A cloud of gray vapor swirled about Meguire's head. "X," holding his breath, received none of the small charge of anesthetizing gas which the cigarette contained. Meguire sagged forward. His eyes were no longer sleepy. They were wide with fright.

"Who — who are you?" he stuttered.

"X" chuckled. "If you knew, you'd die of fright."

But it was doubtful if Meguire heard "X's" scoffing

remark. The anesthetizing gas was already dragging him down. "X" supported the man, carried him across the room, and dumped him into a closet. He closed the door, and entered Meguire's bedroom.

One of Secret Agent "X's" most remarkable traits is his memory. Once he has mastered a disguise, he requires no photographs to recreate it. Seated before a mirror, "X" unfolded his compact makeup kit. He spread pigment and plastic makeup material before him. Then he took out a black toupee. A few minutes of careful work, and he was once again Peter Krausman, wealthy jeweler and receiver of stolen goods.

He was in the act of putting the finishing touches on his makeup, when the front door buzzer sounded. Going out into the hall, "X" spoke into the speaking-tube, imitating the voice of "Sleepy" Meguire to perfection. The real Krausman announced himself, and "X" told him to come up at once.

When Krausman knocked at the door of the apartment, "X" opened quickly, swinging with the panel so that Krausman was inside the room before he had time to see the Agent.

The dusky skin of Peter Krausman paled. For a moment, he could do nothing but stare at this exact counterpart of himself. With a movement that seemed no more than a gesture, "X" drew his gas pistol.

Slowly, the color returned to Krausman's face. "So," he said, "it is true what they say of you — that you can assume any features you choose and impersonate anybody. You are Secret Agent 'X'."

"X" bowed. "I am the reason for your suddenly leaving town yesterday morning."

Krausman frowned. "I do not understand. I was forced to fly to Chicago —"

"To make room for me in your jewelry store," the Agent interrupted. "The game's up, Krausman. When the man who looked like Scar Fassler chose such a convenient means of getting out of your store when he was cornered, I knew that Fassler had been there frequently. Why? Because you associate with Fassler and the rest of the murdering gang that has terrorized the city. You were forced to fly to Chicago, because your chief ordered it. He knew that, since I had been tipped off to the robbery, I would be there. He was hoping that I would choose to appear as Peter Krausman. Your leaving town when you did, made the adoption of your character very easy for me. In that manner, I was marked by your chief."

"My chief! A most fantastic story!" declared Krausman. "You can't prove a word of it."

"That won't be necessary," replied "X." "I intend to search you carefully —"

Krausman's right hand shot toward his coat pocket. "X's" gas gun hissed. For a moment, Krausman's gypsy-like face was clouded with vapor. His dark eyes flickered. He would have fallen to the floor had not the Agent caught him and let him down easily. The threat to search Krausman had brought terror to the jeweler. Evidently, he had something of vital importance concealed on his person. "X's" heart beat high with hope as he knelt beside Krausman. At last he could hope for some key to the identity of the hidden creature who directed the corpse gang.

In another moment, "X" had emptied the jeweler's pockets. Keys, handkerchief, change wallet, and watch — all of these "X" transferred to his own pockets. It was only after searching Krausman's vest that he came upon something that he thought might be important. It was a neatly folded piece of ivory-finished note paper. A delicate feminine hand had penned this little memo:

"Be at my tailor's at 10 P.M."

The words, "my tailor's" implied that the writer of the note was a man — supposedly Krausman. Yet there could be no doubt that a woman had written it. That, coupled with the fact that the appointment was at such a strange hour, made "X" suspicious. Then too, the paper was not the sort a man would pick up in order to make some brief notation. And it had been exactly folded to fit a small envelope. "X" was certain that here was a message that, when correctly interpreted, would reveal the information which Krausman would have risked his life to guard. Perhaps the note had been a summons to a gang meeting. Perhaps it had been written by the green-eyed Leopard Lady.

Because he had long since learned that the correct answer to the most complete riddle was often the simplest one, "X" turned back Krausman's coat. The suit had been tailor made, but there was no identifying mark on the lining.

Agent "X" sighed. There was nothing to do but make a trip to Krausman's office. There, he hoped to find the information he was seeking.

He removed his leather covered medical kit, took out a hypodermic needle, and deftly filled it with a drug of his own concoction. He injected sufficient amounts in both Krausman and Meguire to keep them both unconscious for several hours. After putting the men in separate rooms, he left the apartment. He nodded at the doorman.[12]

"My car," he muttered. "I'm becoming dreadfully absent-minded. I can't remember whether I took a taxi or —"

The doorman smiled. "Your car is at the curb, sir.

---

[12] AUTHOR'S NOTE: This drug employed by "X" has two remarkable properties. It is particularly speedy in its action; and, unlike other drugs, it leaves no bad after-effects. It is one of his most valued accessories.

When you went upstairs a moment ago, you said you would only be a moment."

"To be sure." The Agent pressed a dollar bill into the doorman's hand, and walked slowly toward a green sedan which the doorman had indicated. A moment of experimentation revealed the key which unlocked Krausman's car. Then "X" was heading downtown in the direction of Krausman's store.

PARKING the green sedan in a nearby garage, "X" walked the remaining block to the store. On the way, he was accosted by a ragged little newshawk. "Here's your paper, Mr. Krausman." The boy thrust the sheet beneath the Agent's nose. Evidently, it was Krausman's custom to patronize the boy. "X" gave the lad a quarter, tucked the paper under his arm, and continued on his way.

Entering the store by the front door, "X" spoke to the clerks and hurried to Krausman's office at the rear. Workmen had already replaced the glass in the office door, and "X" could be certain of his privacy. Then he began a diligent search through all of Krausman's records. Krausman, the fence, evidently kept his records separate from those of Krausman, the jeweler. At any rate, Agent "X" could find nothing that would incriminate the man whose identity he had adopted. Going through a sheaf of canceled checks, "X" came upon several which had been made out to Otho Berg, Tailor. "X" looked up Berg's address in the telephone directory, and made a note of it.

He then opened the newspaper he had purchased, and looked at the front page. The first item his eyes met was:

### CORPSE GANG STRIKES AGAIN

A score of people meet death or serious injury as police squad car crashes into office building.

The article went on, telling how once again the death-dealing mystery car with its corpse drivers had prevented the police from getting to the scene of a bank robbery. Fifty thousand dollars had found their way into the grasping fingers of the hidden monster in this latest venture.

According to the paper, an invention of the energetic Major Derrick had given an impartial and perfect record of the police butchering. On the major's suggestion, an automatic camera had been installed in the police car and could be set into operation by anyone in the car. This camera had taken a picture of the mystery car and its two occupants at exactly the moment when the driver of the police car had been killed by machine-gun slugs. The picture had been enlarged so that the faces of the men in the mystery car could be plainly seen. Beneath the picture was printed this question:

### ARE EITHER OF THESE MEN THE NOTORIOUS SECRET AGENT "X"?

This was followed by the announcement made by Commissioner Foster. Fifty thousand dollars would be paid to anyone who would deliver Secret Agent "X" dead or alive to the police. The commissioner went on to say that Agent "X" alone could be responsible for these crimes. "The man," Foster was quoted as saying, "is a genius gone berserk. He must be checked at all costs."

Another boxed-in article dealt with the investigation of the grave of "Slash" Carmody. It had been discovered that the grave had been opened shortly after interment. The casket was found empty. Many were the theories advanced by scientists as to how Carmody might have been brought back to life — for one of the men in the black mystery car was certainly "Slash" Carmody.

In the office of Peter Krausman, Agent "X" smiled

grimly. He had considered each of the theories advanced by men of science, concerning the restoring of life after death. None had guessed the truth. Perhaps Agent "X" was the only living person who understood the method by which the Corpse Legion had been created.

# VII

## ALIAS, THE CORPSE

THE Berg Tailor Shop was hardly more than a hole in the wall, in a little, run-down side street. It was sandwiched in between an old residence that had been transformed into a tea-room, and the smoky-faced limestone front of a bank.

"X" in the disguise of Krausman and driving Krausman's car, circled the block twice, observing every detail. The little show window of the tailor shop was brilliantly lighted and displayed the latest fabrics. The tea-room next door looked innocent enough with its soft rosy lights passing through cheerful, clean windows. The bank was as lifeless as the grave; not a light showed. Its windows were securely barred. For the past year, this bank had been closed. It was the bank of Mr. Stinehope whom "X" had met the day before.

"X" decided that if he was to enter the tailor shop, he must do so from the rear. The front was too brilliantly lighted. He would attract the attention of the cop on the beat in no time if he attempted to pick the lock on the front door.

"X" steered the car around the corner and into the alley. Then he got out, having made certain that no one was watching, and approached the shop. A light was burning in the rear.

Upon a tailor's bench and beneath a dim light, a man sat with his legs crossed under him. His back was toward "X" and his head was bent far over, eyes close to his work. There was nothing whatever to indicate that the shop was to be the scene of a meeting of a ruthless criminal organization. And perhaps it was not. It was possible that "X" had misinterpreted the note he had found in Krausman's pocket. At any rate, there was no turning back now. "X" approached the door, and knocked.

From where he stood, "X" watched the shadow of the man on the tailor's bench unfold and cross the room. In another moment, the door had opened and a soft, husky voice said, "Come in, Mr. Krausman, the coat is ready for fitting."

"X" stared into the face of the man he had seen on the bench. Scarlet lips smiled at him; narrow, acutely slanting brows winked; eyes of emerald green scintillated in the light of the shop.

"Surprised, Peter?" came the query in the unmistakable voice of the Leopard Lady. For the person in male attire who had been seated on the tailor's bench was none other than Felice Vincart. She closed the door, and bolted it behind "X."

"Now, if you'll just slip off your coat, Peter," she whispered, "we'll get on with our work."

"X" glanced about the room. There were three other figures in the shop. In the dim light, they appeared as tailor's dummies, so still did they stand. But their faces were the faces of corpses — criminals who had met their just deserts years ago. Aware that the Leopard Lady was watching him closely, "X" crossed the room, took off his suit coat and tossed it onto a chair. The Leopard Lady helped him into a half finished coat of rough tweed.

"There's work for you to do tonight," said the Leopard Lady softly. She busied herself with chalk and tapeline. "About fifty thousand dollars worth of jewels to dispose of. The chief is getting a little anxious to see them turned into cash. But you'll have to pay a fair price."

"Haven't I always been fair with the chief?" asked "X" in Krausman's voice.

The Leopard Lady nodded. "I was merely warning you. Stand still, can't you? You don't look like a man who's trying on a new suit."

"X" laughed uneasily. "You don't expect me to, do you?"

"She does," one of the criminals who posed as a clothing store dummy said. "She's got ice water in her veins. What's more, she doesn't give a damn. Just does this for a thrill."

The Leopard Lady uttered her purring laugh. "Don't you get a kick out of it, too?" she asked of the "dummy."

"X" saw the man tremble slightly. "Not always," he replied. "X" noticed that the man did not have the peculiar intonation and pronunciation of a creature of the underworld. His voice definitely belied his hard-looking face. Perhaps beneath those coarse features was the face of a man who was considered a distinct asset to society. Or he might be some whitecollar worker whose luck had not lasted, and who had taken up crime as a means of getting rich quick.

"The key to the chief's success," explained the Leopard Lady, "lies in his daring. He planned this meeting here tonight. What could be more simple? No drawn blinds; no black masks. If the cop on the beat should pass this alley window at this moment, he would notice nothing out of the way. Why, I might even ask him in for a smoke."

"Don't try any tricks like that!" said one of the dummies with a shudder.

"And now," said the Leopard Lady, as she helped "X" from the coat, "we'll go into the bank. One of you men stay here. The others follow Krausman and me."

"X" was given no opportunity to regain his own coat. The Leopard Lady led them through a door and into a little room that was without lights or windows. Flashlights, in the hands of the two criminals who followed them, cut through the gloom and centered upon a section of the brick wall. One of the men approached the wall, and tapped out a loose brick. Thrusting his arm into a deep hole in the wall, the man seemed to grasp some sort of a handle.

On well-oiled hinges, a section of the wall, big enough to admit a man, swung outward. Through the opening, "X" saw a wall of metal. An oblong piece had been rimmed by the cutting flame of an acetylene torch. At a touch from one of the gang members, the steel section swung open. Agent "X" was led into the vaults of Mr. Stinehope's own bank.

What better place could the gang have had for a cache for their loot? The bank was closed; its vaults were supposedly empty.

The Leopard Lady knelt before a large safety deposit box, unlocked it, and pulled it open. Inside was a canvas bag. She took the bag out, loosened the drawstrings, and emptied its glittering contents on the floor. "X" knelt beside her, picked up a great handful of rings, bracelets, and necklaces. He let the jewels sift through his fingers, and tinkle against the floor.

"Well, how much?" demanded the Leopard Lady.

"X" hesitated. Though he knew good gems when he saw them, he had no idea of the amount of money a fence would be expected to advance on the lot. "Really," he said, "you can't expect me to make an offer without a day or so to think it over. I will take these with me, and let you know later."

The green eyes of the Leopard Lady were fixed on his face. The narrow brows drew together in a tight frown. "I don't understand, Peter. You have always set the price, and paid cash immediately. Why the hesitation this time? You know that the chief never picks up anything but the very best stuff. Cash is all that he's interested in. He's always treated you fairly."

"X" tugged at the lobe of his left ear. "What did I pay you for the last haul? I am afraid I can't do so well. The risk is tremendous."

One of the criminals laughed. "It must be! And all

you've got to do is dig out the stones, melt the gold, and turn the stuff into new jewelry for which your customers pay triple the price the chief asks."

Felice Vincart placed a slender hand on "X's" coat sleeve. "What did you pay for the last catch, Peter?"

"Twenty thousand, wasn't it?" It was a blind shot. "X" hadn't the slightest idea what the last haul of gems had been worth.

Suddenly, two automatics flashed into prominence. "X" sprang to his feet, but his head was wedged between the muzzles of two guns in the hands of the corpse-faced criminals.

The Leopard Lady's lips twisted into a sneer. "Sometimes you actually disappoint me, Secret Agent 'X!' Keep the guns on his head, men. He probably wears a bulletproof vest. March him back the same way. The chief will be delighted."

Slowly, the group moved to the back of the vault. "X" knew that his slightest move would be stark suicide. One of the criminals stepped through the opening in the wall, pressed a gun to the back of "X's" head, and ordered him to step backward through the opening.

"X" had no choice in the matter. In another moment, he was hurried up the alley, his head still held between two guns. A car awaited them, and with infinite care "X" was forced into the back seat. With a gunman on either side, ready and willing to shoot, he was made to sit stiffly upright. The Leopard Lady slid in under the wheel.

Suddenly, one of the guns was removed from his temple. "X" half turned his head, met blinding white light, felt sickening pain, and lapsed into unconsciousness.

"X" regained his senses in a room that blazed with light. He was sitting in a large oak chair, hands and arms unfettered. Across the room from him, a door was partially hidden by a row of six men, all with the corpse-faces that characterized those associated with the mob of killers. Each man stood stiffly erect, a rifle in his hands.

Standing a little to the left of Agent "X" was a shapeless figure in black. A shroudlike garment covered the creature from head to foot. Only tiny holes for eyes were visible.

"I've grown tired of this nonsense, Agent 'X'," spoke the somber figure. "I had hoped to frame you and put you into police custody. No form of execution can compare with the electric chair. Unfortunately, inasmuch as I am compelled to change headquarters frequently, I cannot carry an electric chair with me. I have decided that you shall be shot as a spy as the clock strikes the hour of nine.

"Nine? Is it morning, then?" asked "X" quietly.

"Yes," replied the gang leader. "You have been unconscious for a number of hours due to the blow you received on the head."

"X" glanced at his watch. The hands spelled a quarter of nine. "Just how do you propose to carry your schemes out without me?" he asked. "If you kill me, you won't have anyone to blame your crimes on. After challenging the police in my name, you can't very well kill me. Obviously, I can't be the man behind the gang if I am dead."

A dull laugh sounded from the shroud. "Fassler, Carmody, and many of the others were dead to police records; yet when I wanted them, they appeared to serve me. With you, the same thing can be accomplished. You have no idea what I did to you with my own hands when you were first brought into my presence."

"On the contrary, I have a very good idea," replied "X". "It was all rather simple for a man of your skill."

"Then you will understand that I no longer need you. I am sorry that our last visit must terminate so abruptly. Breathe deeply, Agent "X". You have now just ten minutes on this earth. A pleasant thought for you to mull over in that time, is that within a month, I shall have probably wiped out the entire police force and become the wealthiest man in the world."

The shrouded figure turned, passed through the line of armed guards. At the door, it paused, turned, and said:

"It would do you no good to cry for help, Agent 'X'. You are in a room that is perfectly soundproof."

Again "X" chuckled grimly. "You rather underestimate my courage."

"Good bye, then." The shrouded figure moved through the door. The panel closing behind him sounded hollowly throughout the room. It was like the closing of a coffin.

To all outward appearances, Secret Agent "X" was perfectly cool. Actually, a righteous hatred consumed him; hatred for the black-clad butcher. For "X" knew that the eyes visible through the arch-criminal's black shroud were the eyes of the one man who had seen "X's" true face. And from what the shrouded one had said, "X" believed that the killer had obtained a permanent record of the Agent's features.

"X" stared straight ahead of him. The squadron of killers opposite him stood like statues, their eyes on the clock above the Agent's head. These strange faces — corpse-faces out of the past — were to haunt him for the rest of his days. They were so cold, so void of every human trait, so filled with an eagerness to destroy life.

"X" looked at his watch. In five minutes — less than that — six guns would blast him into eternity. If he chose to make a break for liberty, the shooting would be less accurate, certainly more painful, with death approaching more slowly but just as inevitably.

But the Agent's brain pounded out: "I dare not die!" So much depended upon his living; and the chances of his living depended upon only one thing — the gold timepiece in his hand. Three minutes until the balance of life and death swung one way or another.

Agent "X" pressed his watch between his palms and unscrewed the back of the case. Beneath, was a second crystal which one might have imagined was placed there to keep dirt and water out of the movement. "X" looked up at the guards. A deceptive smile stole across his lips. "My watch seems to have stopped. Can any of you gentlemen tell me the correct time?"

Each of the corpselike faces grinned. "You aren't going to care," said one of the men.

"Oh, yes," the agent contradicted. "I'm going to care a lot. You see, I'm duty bound to attend a funeral within the next day or so."

One of the guards guffawed. "You're a cool one! Sure, you have got a date with the undertaker, haven't you? Well, I don't imagine there'll be enough of you to bury."

"You misunderstand me," said "X" quietly. "I referred to the first of a series of funerals — the funeral of your leader. I rather imagine he'll go down to stir the fires of hell — a sort of preparation for your descent to the self-same spot."

The agent leaned far forward in the chair. The heavy lips he had affected in his disguise as Peter Krausman remained fixed in a smile of contempt. "You see," he whispered, "I'm going to walk out of here in a few minutes. That's something that I am afraid you will be unable to do as —"

The first stroke of nine boomed throughout the cell. Agent "X" stood up, still smiling. Simultaneously, six rifles were raised to six shoulders. The Agent's right arm swung high up over his head and then came thrashing down. Across the room, a little gold missile flashed. A faint pop and broken glass tinkled on the paved floor. With the agility of an adagio dancer, "X" sprang to the side of the room.

A sharp cry burst from the lips of one of the guards. Rifles wheeled. One of them cracked. Agent "X" dropped face down on the floor, and began rolling toward the door. His breath was locked in his throat. He dared not breathe; for the back of his watch had contained enough anesthetizing vapor under high pressure, to knock out every one in the room in a few moments time.

Another wild shot. The guard who had fired stumbled forward on his knees, then relaxed to the floor. Another sprang to the door and groped ineffectually at the handle. Springing to his feet, "X" wiped the man's feeble hand from the knob, gave him a push that sent him spinning across the room. "X" seized the handle, and yanked open the door. He closed it behind him, found the key in the lock, and twisted it.

For only a moment, he leaned against the door, and sobbed a great lungful of air. He was in the upper hall of a house, the location of which was unknown to him. Through a smeary window, he could look down into an unkempt back yard. The sky was like gray flannel, and the rain fell in a steady drizzle.

At the other end of the hall, "X" saw a narrow stairway leading down into darkness. He moved toward it on tiptoe; for though he might have escaped from the window, he was placing other matters before his own safety. The black-robed butcher was still at large.

Descending the stairs, "X" came upon a closed door. Peering through the keyhole, he discovered that the next room was empty as far as he could see. He cautiously opened the door, and stepped into a small hall. The sound of a muffled voice, coming from behind the door at his right, arrested him. With infinite caution, he worked his way over to the door. Leaning against the frame, he pressed his ear to the panel. He could hear the voice of the shrouded one quite clearly:

"The first thing to attend to," the shrouded one was saying, "is to check the cars. Refuel the roadster. I believe the guns are fully loaded. Felice Vincart has obtained a plan of the bank building. As you know, the steps leading up to the bank will effectively conceal your approach. It is an ideal setup for us. Have no fear that the police will reach you. They will be unable to answer their radio call just as on previous occasions.

"From the bank you will go to that place we have decided upon. It does not pay for us to use the same headquarters for more than two days at a stretch. Even though Agent 'X' is out of the way, there is no reason to be careless. Remember, tomorrow, we pull the trick that will make us rich beyond our wildest dream. And we will have the police on their knees praying for mercy!"

"I hate the coppers," growled a man.

The chief laughed. "You haven't the conception of the word 'hate'!"

Agent "X" waited for no more. That another robbery and police slaughter was being planned was enough to goad him into action. To warn the police would he useless. Every man on the force had a duty to perform, even though it meant certain death. They would answer that radio call, announcing another Corpse-Legion robbery. And they would be butchered by the guns on the mystery car. Upon the shoulders of Secret Agent "X" a heavy responsibility rested.

He hurried back into the kitchen of the old house where the killer had taken up temporary headquarters.

From a window, he determined the location of the garage. It was attached to the side of the house itself. Opening a door off the kitchen, he descended a short flight of steps, and entered the garage. Inside, was a single car — the great, black, streamlined roadster with its mounted machine guns. This was the speed-demon which had spelled destruction for so many brave men.

As he stared over its gleaming length, the agent's breath caught. For a moment, he stood perfectly rigid. There were two men in the car. And "X" was totally without weapons. In another moment, a slow, understanding smile spread over the Agent's face. The man behind the wheel stared straight ahead. The other crouched low behind a machine gun. The man behind the gun was "Slash" Carmody who had been executed a few days before in the electric chair. And no miracle of modern science had altered that fact. Carmody, though posed behind the deadly gun, was still a corpse. So was the man behind the wheel.

"X" had not a moment to lose if he was to carry out the daring plan he had conceived. To cripple the car, jam its machine gun, were both impractical ideas. The mystery car, upon which so much depended, would be given a careful inspection before it started on its juggernaut journey.

"X" rounded the car until he was face to face with the embalmed corpse of Carmody. He had already guessed that Carmody's grave had been robbed by some member of the gang. The fact that the car's occupants were corpses explained why the police bullets had had no effect upon them. There were no less than three neat, bloodless holes drilled in Carmody's forehead.

IN a moment, "X" had opened the car door. The hands of the corpse were taped to the stock of the machine gun. It took "X" only a moment to loosen these bonds, and drag the gruesome, stiffened body from the car.

Looking around for a place to hide the body, he discovered a small washroom, just off the garage. With his grisly burden, he entered the washroom. Then he began the most trying disguise of his career.

From the heels of his shoes, "X" took a small tube of plastic makeup material. The plastic volatile substance which he used to change his features was nearly colorless. He would require no pigment for this impersonation. With a speed that did not sacrifice care, he removed the makeup that identified him as Peter Krausman and quickly altered his features to resemble those of the dead man.

The effect achieved by the pale makeup material was nothing short of horrible. In five minutes time, "X" transformed his face from that of a normal, healthy man, into the immobile, death-sharpened features of a corpse.

Then he had to strip the body, and put on the dead man's suit and hat. He had only time to lock the washroom, pocket the key, and take his place in the black roadster before the garage door opened, and two men entered.

"You got to hand it to the chief," one of the men was saying. "He sure gets the ideas!"

"I'm breathing again now that Agent 'X' is out of the way," said the other. "The chief says he always knew he'd get him." The man was unscrewing the gas tank top in order to inspect the fuel supply. His companion rounded the car and approached the side where "X" sat.

"Well damn me if Slash Carmody hasn't come loose!" he exclaimed. "Somebody removed the tape that held his hands to the gun."

The Agent's heart gave a bound. He had, acting solely from memory assumed the same position as that of the corpse. His hands were on the machine gun, but there had been no way to tape them there.

"Probably," said the other man callously, "the chief had Carmody out for an airing. Here, Smokey —" he tossed a roll of friction tape to the man near "X".

Smokey eyed "X" a little fearfully. "X" stared back, dull-eyed, and unblinking. He knew that if the mobster should touch his flesh and discover that it was warm and living, his daring scheme would come to an abrupt termination.

But Smokey was not a man to fondle a corpse. Gingerly, he pressed the friction tape to the gun and wrapped it securely around "X's" wrists without touching his flesh. When he had completed the job, "X" was securely tied to a machine gun that was fully loaded for its murderous work.

Suddenly, the door from the kitchen opened. On the top of the little flight of steps stood the great shapeless shadow of the gang leader himself.

"Agent 'X' has escaped!" he shouted.

"Escaped? You said he was dead!"

"One of his damned tricks!" the shrouded figure growled. "The duel must begin all over again. But —" he added after a moment's consideration — "that need not stop us. Nothing can stop us. You two join the others in the alley. Drive around in front, and be prepared to leave at once."

The man called Smokey shook his head. "It's a lot of risk to take. Agent 'X' may have warned the police."

The black-clad butcher laughed harshly. "What good would that do? The police believe that 'X' is responsible for the police killings."

"Right, chief! We'll start as soon as I put a little air in this rear tire."

The black-robed one left the garage to his lieutenants. "X" heard the rush of air as the roadster's tires were filled. He dared not move a muscle; for the man called Smokey watched him closely. Was there a glimmer of suspicion in the cold eyes of the killer?

Had "X" been given a moment alone, he could have managed to break away from the bonds that held him to the death car. But no sooner had Smokey and his companion left the garage than "X" felt the car in which he was seated tremble slightly. He darted a look at the corpse at the wheel. Had he been mistaken? Was this stiff, wooden-faced thing alive after all? But the corpse beside him remained motionless.

By an unseen hand, the black roadster started. Garage doors folded back by some concealed mechanism. The destroying black car rolled smoothly from the garage, down a steep drive, and into the street directly in front of a blue sedan. Out of the corner of his eye, "X" saw that the blue sedan was filled with men — men whose faces were the faces of the dead. Once again, the Corpse-Legion had been mobilized for another attack against all that stood for law and order.

"X" fully realized the peril of his position. The roadster was closely followed by the sedan, and the occupants of the latter never moved their eyes from the car in front of them. "X" hadn't a chance in the world of freeing himself from the machine gun as long as those criminals were watching him. They would have shot him down at the first movement. No, he had impersonated a corpse. He knew that unless the odds should suddenly shift in his favor he would be a corpse inside of a few minutes. He was caught between two fires. The police would unhesitatingly shoot him on sight; the gangmen following the roadster would shoot him if he made a move.

The mystery car moved smoothly ahead. The steering wheel in the hands of the corpse remained motionless, though the car negotiated turns easily enough.

The roadster gained speed. It was heading toward a part of the city where many factory workers dwelt. No doubt the objective was some bank where hard working men and women stored the savings of a lifetime.

Staring straight ahead over the long hood of the car, "X" saw the rear end of a special police cruiser. Suddenly, the siren of the police car began to whine. It wheeled to the center of the street, and fairly leaped ahead. "X" ventured a look behind. The blue sedan no longer followed. Evidently, it had speeded ahead to the bank that was to be robbed. The ever-alert police had heard the alarm and were rushing to the scene of the crime.

But if the police car seemed to leap, the black roadster seemed to have suddenly begot wings. Its powerful motor abruptly opened up. The acceleration was so great that "X" felt as though his head would be snapped from his shoulders. The distance between the black destroyer and its prey shortened alarmingly.

But Agent "X" was not idle. He knew the hidden hand that guided the car would open up the machine gun as soon as the roadster overhauled the police car. He knew, also, that police guns would send a hail of lead that "X", in his position in the roadster, could not possibly avoid. The powerful muscles of the Agent's arms swelled until it seemed that his skin must burst. There was a sound of ripping fabric as he broke through the friction tape which held him to the gun.

As his hand pulled free, a great shout arose from the police car. They had sighted the roadster that was overtaking them. One of the police leaned far out and sent a shot whining above the Agent's head. There were few people on the street, and the police would have no reason to hold their fire; they would shoot to kill.

The Agent's hands worked like lighting, tugging at the clasp that held the ammunition drum of the machine gun in place. The clasp yielded. He fastened both hands on the drum, and yanked it free. He hurled it into the street. At the same time, police automatics barked. A slug thudded against "X's" bulletproof vest. He could not hope to be that fortunate always; one of those hungry pellets must find his head.

Staring down, he saw the pavement, a speeding ribbon beneath him. To leap meant — But where was the choice? Without a moment's hesitation, "X" swung one leg over the door of the roadster. A bullet sliced across the calf of his leg and spanged against the armor plate body of the roadster. The Agent's body rocked. He was thrown completely off balance. His arms shot out in a mighty heave that threw him off into space. He had a sickening sensation, as though he were being hurled off of a spinning planet. He was running before he touched the pavement, but it would have been impossible for him to time his pace with that of the roaring, speeding roadster.

His legs doubled under him. He rolled like a ball. A slug imbedded itself in the asphalt not more than an inch from his head. His left shoulder encountered the curb with such force that his entire left arm went suddenly dead.

But he was on his feet, dizzy with the speed of his fall, and momentarily sick with pain. He ran as he had never run before. It was something more than the thought of what might happen to him if he were caught that gave him strength. He was urged on by that exhilaration that comes to a man after he has attempted the impossible and succeeded. For the first time, the terror car was crippled. This time, the killer could not kill.

Swinging in an alley toward a haven of refuge that he knew of, the depressing thought returned to "X" — while he had saved a carload of police and possibly thousands of dollars, the master criminal remained at large. The thought that this monster knew the Agent's true face hung like a Sword of Damocles above his head.

What would be the shrouded monster's next move?

He asked the question, dreading the answer.

# *VIII*
## NIGHT ATTACK

THE following afternoon, the newspapers made gratifying reading for the thousands who lived in fear of the corpse gang. Crippled by the loss of its machine-gun ammunition, the mystery car had had to beat a speedy retreat. The corpse gang, in the act of looting the bank, heard the whine of the police car siren coming nearer and nearer. When it was not interrupted by the rattle of machine-gun fire, the entire crowd took to its heels, narrowly escaping with a few dollars loot.

The police were at last making definite progress, the papers said. But Commissioner Foster silently shook his head. As far as he knew, the failure of the black roadster to wreck the police car was due to carelessness on the part of some one in the criminal group. He felt none of the sense of security returning to him. The Corpse-Legion would strike again and again. He knew of the dogged determination of Secret Agent "X", who he still believed backed the Corpse-Legion.

It was nine o'clock that evening when Commissioner Foster entered the apartment of Major Derrick, his friend and advisor. Little did Foster know that one minute later, a shadow slipped across the front of the apartment building to enter a telephone booth in a neighboring drug store. Calling a number that was listed in no telephone book, the man who had shadowed the commissioner spoke briefly:

"Foster entered Derrick apartment."

In a small, poorly furnished little room in an old brick-faced dwelling several miles away, a grave-faced man listened to that announcement over the phone. "Good!" he whispered. "And where is Burks?"

"Last report stated Inspector Burks in headquarters office looking over reports."

The grave-faced man quietly hung up. Here, in this poor tenement, Secret Agent "X" had established one of his many hideouts. It had been a busy day for him. Through him, a tip had reached police headquarters as to the location of the building where "X" had been forced to face a firing squad. In the disguise of a policeman, "X" had taken part in a raid that had netted the police nothing. The wily creature whose identity was always hidden beneath a shroud had moved his headquarters immediately after the frustration of his bank-robbing scheme by Agent "X".

"X" had then repaired to this tenement hideout where he had been in close touch with Bates and his agents. Various suspects had been carefully watched, but aside from "Sleepy" Meguire's visit to a one-time speakeasy, there was nothing to arouse suspicion.

As soon as he had hung up the phone, Agent "X" went about creating another of his masterful disguises. This time, under his magic fingers, the grave, gray face which he had affected all afternoon gave place to the plump, rosy face of Inspector John Burks. It was one of his most daring simulations, yet one which had gained him valuable information many times before.

"X" left the tenement and went to a garage where a car was waiting for him. It was a roadster with the letters "P.D." lacquered on both doors.

A quarter of an hour later, "X" pulled up in front of the apartment where Major Derrick lived. In a moment, imitating the voice of John Burks to perfection, he announced himself through the speaking-tube which led to Derrick's rooms. He was told to come up at once.

"What's on your mind, Inspector?" Foster demanded, when "X" put in his appearance.

"Plenty!" retorted the Agent. "I've got a straight tip, commissioner. Dope on this corpse gang. If the tip's okay, it'll knock you over!"

"If it's okay," remarked Foster skeptically.

Major Derrick spread his nostrils, and sniffed sharply. "There's been so many false leads lately, inspector, I'm beginning to get discouraged."

"You know Stinehope, the banker?" asked "X".

Both men nodded.

"Then come along. We're going to pick up Stinehope, and go out to his bank."

"The bank's been closed for a long time," declared Foster.

"You don't know that Stinehope's connected with this crew, do you?" Derrick demanded,

"X" shrugged. "Stinehope's bank has failed. But — well, do you see what I mean?"

Derrick nodded gravely. "He doesn't seem to be hurt financially, does he? With you in a moment. The sky looks threatening." Derrick hurried into the next room to reappear a little later carrying a raincoat. "Right, gentlemen. On our way."

TEN minutes later, the Agent's fake police car, carrying the commissioner and his friend, pulled up in front of the Stinehope mansion. Derrick climbed into the rumble seat with Foster. "X" went up to the Stinehope house to get the banker.

"I am afraid I don't quite understand, inspector," said the small, thoughtful-faced Mr. Stinehope when "X" informed him that he must come with him.

"I believe you will when we reach the bank," said "X" gruffly.

"The bank? Why, no banks are open at this time of the night!"

"This one's open twenty-four hours a day!"

The Agent waited for Stinehope to get his hat; then taking him by the arm, led him out to the car.

As the banker began to realize the direction the car

was taking, he was seized with a violent fit of trembling. From his position at the wheel, "X" watched him surreptitiously. "Matter, Stinehope?" he asked.

"Where are we going?"

"To your bank," said the Agent, "I want you to see something."

"X" drove the police car into the alley, and stopped behind Otho Berg's tailoring shop. The place was dark, but the door yielded to one of "X's" master keys.

"You've a search warrant?" asked Foster, who was a stickler for police routine.

"X" nodded. He had nothing of the sort, but he knew that he was not likely to run up against any opposition from the owner of the shop. He had checked up on Berg. The man was above reproach and half blind from his years at the bench. It was little wonder that the corpse mob had been able to construct the secret door leading from the tailor shop into the bank vault. Probably, they had worked only at late hours of the night.

After a few minutes of perfectly unnecessary search, "X" found the secret opening in the brick wall. "Now," he said, "we enter the closed and supposedly empty vault of Mr. Stinehope's bank."

"I tell you, sir, this is the most surprising thing I have ever witnessed!" declared Stinehope.

"That may be," replied "X" dryly. He pointed out the place where the steel wall of the vault had been cut by the acetylene torch.

"Amazing!" cried Derrick as "X" pushed through the steel panel and entered the vault.

Commissioner Foster was speechless.

"Got the master key to these safety deposit boxes?" asked "X" of Stinehope.

"N-no," the banker stuttered. "They are in my office in the next room. But what you expect to find, is beyond me. These boxes have all been emptied —"

"Get the keys," the Agent cut in. "This vault probably contains the cash which was lifted by the corpse gang. Can't this vault be opened from the inside?"

Stinehope nodded. "After one of our clerks was nearly suffocated inside this vault, I installed an electric lock operating from the inside as a safety measure." He approached the great circular door, touched a button on the lock mechanism, and threw his weight against the door.

As Stinehope was about to leave the vault, Foster seized Derrick's arm, whispered: "Don't let Stinehope out of your sight!"

Stinehope was crossing the room toward what had once been his office. Derrick nodded, and ran on ridiculously short legs to Stinehope's side.

Foster turned to the Agent. "Where did you get this information, inspector?"

"From Secret Agent 'X'" replied the Agent

Foster frowned. "I don't understand —"

"Naturally. Secret Agent 'X' is a much misunderstood man, commissioner. He's done some queer things, but he doesn't happen to be the head of the Corpse-Legion. Some one is impersonating him."

Was there a look of suspicion in Foster's eyes? "X" knew that he skated on thin ice. Foster knew of the Agent's many disguises. At one time, "X" had actually impersonated the commissioner himself.

"You see," the Agent explained quickly, "anyone could impersonate Agent 'X'. Had you thought of that? Since 'X' seems to have a limitless number of faces, each of which he wears equally well —"

A cry of stark terror echoed and re-echoed throughout the chamber. The front door of the building had suddenly been thrown open. With deadly machine guns bristling, a small army of men advanced — men whose faces were faces of men long since dead. With silent, terrifying swiftness the Corpse-Legion advanced into the room.

With the quickness of a cat, Major Derrick sprang toward a small elevator cage. He dragged the paralyzed banker behind him. He flung back the door, threw Stinehope inside, and followed. Two of the mobsters leaped toward the elevator. Derrick knocked over the starting lever and at the same time drew his automatic. His was the first shot, fired from the rapidly ascending cage.

Foster drew a gun and dropped behind a marble counter. "X" was beside him in a moment, flattening himself on the floor just as a sub-machine gun began its hateful rattle. Slugs drilled jagged holes in the marble facing of the counter. Agent "X's" powerful hand was over the commissioner's head, pressing him flat to the floor. But a fraction of an inch separated them from the searing line of lead from the machine gun. One of the pellets burned across the Agent's hand, drawing blood.

"Not a sound," the Agent warned. "We haven't a chance against that mob."

Came the sound of feet pelting up the stair. "X" knew that an effort was being made to cut off Stinehope and Derrick. He raised his head ever so slightly, peering through one of the jagged holes drilled by machine-gun fire. One of the corpse-faced criminals guarded the front door. Two more were tiptoeing toward their hiding place, guns ready for instant use.

"X" nudged Foster. "Back! Work your way back to the vault. It's our only chance. I'll hold them back until you get clear."

"Like hell!" Foster muttered between clenched teeth. "I'll stick with you!"

"Right! We'll move toward the vault together." The Agent's hand went to his pocket, and closed over a small metal cartridge. "Turn around, Foster," he directed. "Get the position of that vault in your mind. Close your eyes, and go for it. I've got a tear gas bomb here that will fix 'em."[13]

"Got it!" whispered Foster. "Let go the gas!"

"X" had already snaked his way toward the end of the counter. Suddenly, his arm shot out around the corner of the counter. There was a faint pop, a hiss, and immediately the acrid fumes of the gas started to spread. "X" scrambled to his feet. There came the *rat-tat-tat* of a machine gun-wild, aimless shots that tore jagged slivers from the floor beneath his feet. Though his eyes were streaming from the effects of the gas, "X" made out Foster's stumbling form.

The commissioner was yards from the door of the vault. "X" sprang to him, seized him by the small of the back, and shoved him into the vault.

It required all of his strength to yank the door shut behind them.

He leaped to the end of the vault, and pulled open the secret door. A shadow flitted across the interior of the tailor shop. There was the sound of heavy breathing. A door opened for an instant and closed. The sound of feet running up a metal stairway. "X" leaped through the opening, drawing his gas gun. For a moment, the light from a window flashed across a cruel, noxious face. One of the corpse-criminals had been sent to cut off their escape. Orange-red gun flame slashed through the gloom.

---

[13] AUTHOR'S NOTE: Probably, Agent "X" employed tear gas here, rather than a bomb containing his anesthetizing vapor, because tear gas is recognized by the police as an orthodox weapon. It must be remembered that when "X" assumes a disguise, he immediately identifies himself with the character of the man he represents. Foster, who has met Agent "X" many times, would have certainly known that the man who accompanied him was not Inspector Burks if "X" had used some strange weapon, rather than tear gas.

"X" dropped flat, rolled to one side and encountered a chair. His legs doubled, shot out, sending the chair spinning across the room toward the place from which the gun-shot had come. The man fired at the moving chair. On his feet, "X" leaped toward the shadowy figure. He landed full weight upon the man's back. His left arm crooked around the killer's neck. His right clawed darkness, searching for the man's gun.

Together, they crashed to the floor. "X's" hand slid along the killer's right arm, and met an automatic. With a powerful wrench, he disarmed the man, gripped the automatic, and drove it hard against the man's head. The killer suddenly relaxed. On his feet again, "X" called:

"Foster, where are you?" He pulled out his flashlight, sending the spear of light through the gloom toward the secret door of the vault. His face pale, but his jaw firmly set, Foster sprang through the opening.

"Burks, are you hurt?"

"Not a scratch. This way!" The Agent seized Foster's arm and dragged him to the back of the shop and through the open door into the alley. "Get to a call box, and sound an alarm. The chief killer was here tonight! Get the boys here at once —"

Suddenly, air near the Agent's face was violently fanned. An oath stumbled from Foster's lips. There was a hideous flopping sound as something struck the pavement near at hand. The Agent's flash performed an arc and came to rest upon a horrible black blot on the alley pavement. A human being had been hurled from the sky to certain destruction. Foster dropped to his knees beside the man — a smallish man wearing a dark suit.

"Derrick!" Foster cried. He seized the shoulders of the corpse, turned it over. Blond hair was matted with blood; bone and cartilage had been crushed. The face was a pulpy mass of crimson. "Derrick!" Foster held the battered thing tenderly. His white face was set in a mask of pain. He shook his fist at the black sky above.

"Thrown out of the window!" Agent "X" gritted. "I'm going up, sir." He ran to the back of the building. The lower flight of the fire-escape had been raised by means of counter-balance weights. "X" launched himself in a upward leap. His grasping fingers caught the lower step of the fire escape, dragged it down. Above him, yellow light filtered through one window. "X" took the steps three at a time until he came to the office floor. From the fire-escape, he stared into the deserted office.

A chair had been tipped over; the panel of the door had been splintered. "X" climbed over the sill and approached an untidy desk. There lay a piece of paper upon which a message had been scrawled. "X" picked up the note and read:

> Dear Foster:
> Can't possibly imagine why I never thought of the lucrative practice of kidnapping. How much do you think Mrs. Stinehope will pay for the return of her husband? Am leaving Derrick to you.

The note was signed, "Secret Agent 'X'."

"X" crushed the piece of paper and thrust it into his pocket. Then he returned to the window. Outside sounded the scream of sirens. "X" realized that there was nothing more for him to do there. He returned by the way he had come, anxious to avoid the police lest the real Inspector Burks should be among them.

At the bottom of the fire escape, he found Foster waiting for him. Some of the newly arrived police were carrying the mangled body of Derrick into the bank building. There were no signs of the corpse-criminals.

"I have a grave matter to discuss with you, Burks," said Foster, taking hold of "X's" arm. "We must leave here at once. Come along to the car."

Wondering what was on the commissioner's mind, "X" returned with Foster to the bogus police car.

"You remember Sergeant Dale?" Foster inquired as "X" started the motor.

"X" nodded. "His kid, Betty, was left alone when he died. Betty works on the *Herald*. Nice girl."

"That's the trouble," said Foster slowly. "I can't fathom it. I have just received information that Betty Dale is to be placed under arrest!"

For a moment, Agent "X" was too amazed to speak. Then he forced a laugh. "Good Lord, she couldn't have done anything!"

"There was another police killing this afternoon. A small jewelry store was held up. Another police squad car was riddled with machine-gun bullets from that damnable black mystery car. That ingenious camera device, which poor Derrick invented to take pictures of the occupants of the mystery car, had a different story to tell this time. A blonde woman was behind that murdering machine gun. She has been positively identified as Betty Dale. Knowing what I think of Betty Dale, the information was withheld for some time. What do you suggest?"

"X" hesitated a moment. At the next corner, he turned abruptly to the right. "We'll head for Miss Dale's apartment at once," he said. "If it has to come to an arrest, I think it would be better if you and I, both her friends, handled it on the quiet. It's my opinion that there's a trick somewhere."

"A camera doesn't lie," said Foster softly.

"No, but there's many a trick up the photographer's sleeve," the Agent persisted.

And for the remainder of the distance, both men were silent.

Having mounted the steps to Betty's room, Foster and Agent "X" found Betty at her typewriter. She was frankly amazed at this late visit from the police commissioner and the man she thought to be Inspector Burks. Cordially, she invited them to enter her tidy living room.

"To what do I owe this pleasure?" she asked as she passed a small coffer of cigarettes.

Foster fidgeted and looked at "X". Secret Agent "X" was staring at the toes of his shoes. Foster drew a long breath. "The truth is, Miss Dale, that is, I'm afraid you're in trouble."

A smile melted from the girl's face. Her lovely blue eyes widened. "Just what sort of trouble, commissioner?" she asked.

"What were you doing this afternoon about four o'clock?"

"Why, I was in my car going out to cover an assignment."

"Anyone with you?" Secret Agent "X" asked hopefully.

Betty shook her head without hesitation.

"Miss Dale, you were seen driving a black, streamlined roadster — the machine gun mounted roadster of this corpse gang," Foster broke out.

A puzzled frown crimped Betty's forehead. She laughed a little weakly. "Surely you are not serious!"

"So serious," said Foster, "that there's a warrant out for your arrest on the charge of murder. Things look pretty black for you. At headquarters, they have a picture which clearly shows you crouching behind the machine gun which sent four policemen and two pedestrians to their deaths."

Betty dropped into a chair. For a moment, she remained silent. Then:

"I hardly know what to say. There's been some terrible mistake somewhere. I would like very much to see that picture."

Foster stood up. "May I use your phone? I think it would be easier for all of us if we thrashed this matter out right here. I'll have one of the boys bring that picture right over. If there's been a mistake, you'll find that we are just as anxious to get things straightened out as you are." Foster walked over to Betty's small desk, picked up the phone.

Agent "X" sought Betty's face. Then he glanced over at the commissioner. Foster's back was toward them. The Secret Agent raised his hand, and drew the letter "X" in the air with his forefinger.

Betty took a deep breath. It was like a sob of relief. New color flooded her face. "X" pressed a finger to his lips.

"Hello. Police headquarters?" Foster was speaking. "This is Commissioner Foster. Connect me with the Homicide Bureau." Foster waited. He turned his head to smile hopefully at Betty.

Though there was no outward indication, every nerve in Agent "X's" body was taut as a drawn steel wire. After a seemingly endless moment, Foster turned back to the phone.

"Foster speaking," said the commissioner brusquely. "Regarding that picture taken of the blonde woman behind the machine gun in the mystery car. Would you send that over to Miss Dale's apartment? . . . Hello. Who is this speaking, please?"

"X" shifted his weight forward in the chair.

"Say that again!" Foster whipped out. "You are Inspector Burks?" The commissioner forked the receiver, and pivoted. His hand streaked toward his coat pocket.

# IX

## SHADOW OF THE SHROUD

BUT at the first inflection of doubt in the commissioner's voice, Agent "X" had sprung to his feet. Before he could touch his gun, Foster found himself staring into the Agent's gas gun.

"You — you are Secret Agent 'X'!" Foster accused.

"I am Secret Agent 'X'. Though I hate to remind a man of any favor I have done him, you will always remember me as the man who saved your life tonight. Right now — sleep, and forget."

The gas gun in "X's" hand hissed like a snake. A puff vapor wreathed the commissioner's face. Foster choked, staggered forward, and fell into the Agent's arms. Agent "X" shifted his grip, lifted the commissioner bodily, and walked through the door into Betty's bedroom. He stretched Foster out on the bed, then returned to Betty.

The girl was obviously ill at ease. "I was so afraid for a moment that you were caught," she whispered. "It would have been terrible, terrible to watch them take you away!"

"X" smiled cheerfully. "Poor Foster! He looked a bit helpless, didn't he. But I admire the man. He's a human being clear through. But put on your hat, Betty. You can't stay here. The real Inspector Burks is probably on his way here now. He'll have the warrant and that picture."

Betty paled slightly. "You — you don't think I had anything to do with it?"

"X" laughed heartily. "Bless your heart! Of course, you didn't. But we can't have you spending the night in jail. Rival papers would fry the *Herald* plenty with their star reporter in prison."

"But what does it all mean?"

"X" grew suddenly serious. "It means that you and I are in the tightest place we ever have been in. The criminal behind the corpse-gang not only calls himself Agent 'X', but he imitates my own methods. After the robbery at the Krausman store, what did you do, Betty?"

Standing in front of a mirror, Betty was adjusting her hat. "X" thought that he had never seen anything so beautifully appealing as the reflection in that mirror. Then Betty spoke.

"I went out and got in a taxi. I was acting according to your instructions — to leave as soon as possible. The taxi driver took me a little way in the direction of my apartment. Then he stopped, turned around, and confronted me with a gun. I think I cried out, but before I knew anything else, he had struck me on the head."

THE Agent's steely eyes flashed. "And how long were you unconscious before you awoke in the house of leopards?"

"I've no idea. When I came to, I was too frightened to think."

"Did you notice if your face felt stiff and dry?" the Agent asked.

"Now that you mention it, I believe it did."

"X" nodded, took the girl's arm and steered her through the door. "You see," he whispered as he led her toward the stairway, "this killer has been fighting me with my own weapons. I noticed the same dry feeling on my face when I came to in his prison cell. It was caused by the material he uses in making the masks."

"You mean that while I was unconscious, some one made a mask from my face? Then — then you —"

"X" nodded grimly. "A mask of some sort to get all the features. That enables him to re-create, in a flexible material, the exact counterpart of anyone's features."

"But your face — your real face. Has he seen it?"

"Undoubtedly. What is more, he has a record of it in one of those masks. He's saving it for a coup. That is why this leader of the corpse-legion is the most dangerous man I have ever met."

Outside, "X" opened the door of the police car. "I'm driving you to a friend's house. There's a woman there who can be thoroughly trusted. She is one of my agents. You must stay with her until the skies clear. And don't worry, Betty."

The following afternoon "X" received a communication from Bates that sent the blood coursing a little swifter through his arteries. Another robbery, another brutal police killing had been enacted. But this time, the patient, searching eyes of "X's" own intelligence force had been on the look-out. One of the Agent's own planes, equipped with a moving-picture camera, had followed the course taken by the mystery car. It was little wonder that the mystery car always seemed to vanish into thin air.

The aerial camera had traced the black destroyer along its course, into the mouth of an alley where it had met a huge moving van. A retractable incline had been lowered from the truck, awaiting the mystery car. The black roadster had bumped up the incline and into the van. The incline had been withdrawn, the doors of the van closed. Then the van lumbered from the alley, apparently going about its legitimate business.

But the aerial camera had not stopped there. It had recorded the movement of the van, tracing it through crooked streets until it backed up against a garage coupled with an apparently deserted brick building in the west end of town. Further checking had furnished the address of that house. It was leased in the name of Steven Pyke.

Consulting his records, "X" learned that Pyke had been a smalltime crook who had been out of prison for five years and had apparently gone straight.

Half an hour after he had received this important information from Bates, Agent "X" sauntered down the street on which the Pyke house was situated. He wore the shabby garments of a day laborer. Grease and dirt stained his face. A blue denim cap was pushed back from iron-gray hair.

"X" walked past the Pyke house, apparently without paying any attention to it. Then he rounded the corner of the block, and continued walking until he came to the alley.

He entered the alley and proceeded slowly along, apparently concerned only with the contents of the ash barrels along the route. When he reached the back of the Pyke house, he stopped, and dug around a pile of tin cans with a stick he carried. He lingered there until a woman, who was beating rugs in the yard behind a neighboring house, went inside. Then he approached the door of the garage which was attached to the big brick house.

It required but a moment for him to unlock the door with one of his master keys. He stepped inside, and closed the door behind him. The room which he had entered was a large one. There was room for three cars. However, at present it was occupied only by the black, streamlined roadster which had terrorized the city. The two embalmed corpses were artfully posed in the seat of the car.

"X's" eyes hurried around the garage, paying particular attention to the floor. At length, he tiptoed to the roadster, dropped on hands and knees and looked beneath the car. On the floor beneath was a flat steel plate that looked as though it covered a pit intended for draining oil from the car. Flat on the floor, "X" wormed himself beneath the mystery car until he could reach the steel plate in the floor. He hooked his fingers on the edge of the plate and pushed it forward. It moved easily on oiled guides. As "X" had expected, an oil draining pit was concealed beneath the plate. "X" rolled over the edge of the pit and dropped to the sunken floor below.

He beamed his flashlight over the walls of the narrow pit. Nothing escaped his keen eyes. Everything seemed to indicate that here was an oil drain pit and nothing else. However, "X" noted that a green-painted cabinet attached to the wall was considerably larger than was necessary to hold automobile wrenches. He opened the green door of the cabinet. Four shelves held as many tools. He tapped gently on the back of the cabinet. He felt sure that he would find an opening behind it. His sensitive fingers hurried about the inside of the cabinet, searching for some sort of a concealed spring.

It was only after lifting an extra heavy pipe wrench that he understood the mechanism; for in lifting the wrench, the shelf upon which it rested raised slightly, releasing a hidden latch. "X" pushed on the back of the cabinet. Shelves and all swung inward on well oiled hinges. He stepped through the opening into a rough-walled, narrow passage.

His flashlight lanced ahead. "X" saw that the earth-walled corridor widened only a few feet ahead into a tiny room. Here, uneven timbers formed rough walls that extended in a chimneylike shaft through the basement, and into the upper part of the house. A rude bunk was fastened to one wall. On the other wall several black, shroudlike garments hung on hooks.

Probably, "X" thought, this room was known only to the leader of the gang. Here, he could adopt the black, shapeless garment which identified him. Then an audacious scheme occurred to Agent "X". He took down one of the shroudlike garments, draped it over his head and shoulders, and tied it in place with the black cord provided. Eyeholes cut in the cloth enabled him to see perfectly. No disguise could have been more difficult to penetrate; none could be more simple.

"X" located a rude ladder nailed to the wall and

extending up the shaft into the house. He climbed it quickly to bump his head against the floor above. For a moment, he remained stationary, listening. But he could hear no sound. Very slowly, he pushed up against a trapdoor until his eyes were level with the floor. He was looking into what appeared to be a large closet. He pushed open the trapdoor more fully, and crawled inside. He unlocked the door of the closet — it latched on the inside — and stepped into the room beyond.

Agent "X" froze. A man sat in a chair directly in front of him. The man's head was hidden behind a newspaper. Evidently, he had not heard "X" enter. Beneath the black robe, "X's" hands found his gas gun. He held it ready for immediate use. He coughed slightly.

The man in the chair dropped the newspaper and leaped to his feet. He was a narrow-headed man with a thin, twisted nose, and a receding chin. "X" recognized him immediately as Steve Pyke — a little older than when "X" had last seen him, and perhaps more worldly wise than when he had entered prison some years ago.

"Cripes, chief, someday you're goin' to send me into a panic! I didn't hear you come in. You're about five minutes early. When do we start for Memorial Hall?"

To the best of his ability, "X" recalled the voice of the gang chief. "There is no need to hurry," he replied, evading Pyke's question the best he could . . . Memorial Hall! "X" recalled an announcement he had seen in the paper. The famous antique treasures from the monastic shrines of the city of Kiev, Russia, were to be exhibited in Memorial Hall. The Soviet Government, as a good will gesture, was sponsoring the exhibit in the city. Aside from the value of the treasures from an antique collector's viewpoint, nearly everything in the exhibit was fashioned from purest gold and set with precious stones. The exhibition was to open that night for the benefit of a large number of wealthy art collectors. With the price of gold soaring, it was just the sort of thing that would attract the corpse-gang.

"Sure hope you know what you're doin', chief," Pyke went on. "I don't get it. You say you warned the police? Now if the hall's filled with police, how do you expect to pick up all that gold stuff?"

"Do you question my ability?"

Pyke paled slightly. "No. But there was one time when things went haywire — that time Agent "X" turned up behind the machine gun in the robot car."

"Do not worry about Agent 'X'," he said to Pyke. "Step a little closer and I will tell you exactly what I intend to do with him."

Pyke obeyed a little reluctantly. "X" tossed aside the folds of the black garment he wore. The snout of the gas gun menaced Steve Pyke. Pyke opened his mouth, but the cry of terror choked in his throat as "X" directed a full charge of gas straight into the man's face. Pyke's knees melted under him, and he sagged to the floor.

Then "X" carried Pyke into the closet which served as an outlet for the gang leader's secret passage. There he found a small mirror, and propping the unconscious man against the wall, "X" took off the black garment, took his makeup kit from his pocket, and began another transformation.

Never had his skillful fingers moved so rapidly. He did not know but that at any minute, the real leader of the gang would put in an appearance. Plastic volatile material, pigments of his own concoction, worked together to make simulated flesh and features in perfect imitation of Pyke's face. He replaced the gray wig he wore with a slick brown toupee. Time was passing rapidly. He dared not look at his watch. He must yet change clothes with Pyke, and find some means of concealing the unconscious man.

It required exactly three minutes to effect the change of clothes. A folding-into-the-wall bed in the next room offered a place in which to conceal Pyke. "X" took a last look in the mirror to make certain that his makeup was beyond reproach.

There came a knock at the door. "X" crossed to the panel, turned the key — to admit not the shrouded leader, but Felice Vincart. She was followed by a retinue of the corpse-faced criminals. The Leopard Lady crossed the room with a graceful, catlike tread. Her green eyes flashed at "X". For a moment, he was afraid that those strange eyes must pierce his disguise.

"I have a message from our leader," Felice Vincart purred. "He has been detained. He awaits information concerning the activities of Secret Agent 'X'. He does not want to move until he is certain that 'X' will be in Memorial Hall. It is his intention that 'X' shall die along with Foster, Burks, and others associated with the law.

"We are all to proceed exactly as planned. You, Pyke, will go first, entering the building through the basement door before the guests of the evening are admitted into that part of the building where the exhibit is to be held. It will be your duty to assist with the distribution of the monoxide. The rest of the group will enter the building after the gas has done its work. You, Pyke, shall kill the custodian of the building. You will find him in the basement."

"Let me get this straight," said one of the men behind Felice Vincart. "We're to go into that treasure house after it's been filled with poison gas?"

The Leopard Lady's glittering eyes flashed upon the speaker. "You will all be provided with gas masks. You will be the only living things in the hall. The chief has selected carbon monoxide gas because of all gases it is the most treacherous. It has neither color nor odor. It will simply put everyone in the building to sleep before they know it. It will be a sleep from which there is no awakening.

"Now, go at once. Pyke, you will probably meet our leader in the basement of the building. A car is waiting for you outside the front door. Do not return to this house. It will be abandoned after tonight. You all know of our next meeting place."

Rubbing shoulders with death-faced killers, "X" moved through the door, and into a large reception hall. There, the gang idled, waiting, evidently for the gas masks they were to wear. But "X" was free to leave the building.

He went out the front door, and entered a small coupe that had evidently been provided for his use. He drove down the street, turning the next corner on two wheels, pushing the little car to its best. He drove apparently without thought as to destination. Actually, he was winding a trail that he was certain could not be followed.

He braked the coupe in front of a drug store, got out, and entered a telephone booth. There, he called the Hobart Detective Agency.

"Hello, Jim," he said, using the voice of A. J. Martin, a newspaper man, for it was only in this character that Hobart knew his chief. "I want you to meet a man by the name of Steve Pyke in the basement of Memorial Hall. Get there as soon as possible. Pyke is a man with a thin nose, receding chin, and dark brown hair licked back. Obey him in everything. This is very important."

He waited only for Hobart's cheerful: "Okay." Then he was out in the street, into the coupe, and speeding toward Memorial Hall.

# X

## BENEATH THE SHROUD

A SMALL cement court backed the great brick and limestone building that was Memorial Hall. The arched windows of the hall were tinted with soft lights. A string ensemble was tuning up in the ballroom where, in glass cases, reposed a king's ransom in the wealth of bygone days.

Chalices, altar pieces, elaborately wrought icons, all worked in precious metals and incrusted with priceless jewels, were exhibited for the first time outside of the ancient Russian churches.

Agent "X" drove the coupe into the court. Before he could get out, a man sprang from a shadowy corner and challenged him. Light from the dash of the car revealed the man's features. "X" recognized him as Malvern, one of Inspector Burks' best detectives. Yet there was something about the expression in the man's eyes that was entirely unlike Malvern.

A nervous laugh came from the man's lips. "Oh, it's you, Pyke!"

The voice was vaguely familiar to "X." It was certainly not the voice of Detective Malvern.

"What's the idea?" Agent "X" asked as he swung out of the car.

"Chief's orders," whispered the other. "I'm taking the place of a detective who is suffering from lead poisoning at the moment. You and two others are the only ones to be admitted through this back door."

"X" nodded. "Show me the way."

The man who was disguised as Malvern led the way to a door opening in the foundation of the building. He thrust a key into the lock, and opened the door. Ahead was a darkened stairway. "X's" hand went to his pocket, closed over the butt of his gas pistol.

"Look here, you," he said, when the man had opened the door.

The man turned around, startled by the change of tone in the Agent's voice. "X's" gun nosed over the edge of his pocket. He pulled the trigger. Gas hissed into the man's face. His evil eyes flickered. He would have cried out, but at such short range he had received a considerable quantity of the anesthetizing vapor.

He staggered backward against the wall, then slid down to the pavement. For a moment, the Agent crouched over him. His fingers felt the man's cheeks. They had the resilience of rubber. The man's face was completely covered with a thin, flexible mask duplicating the features of Malvern to perfection.

The flexible material peeled away easily enough, and for a moment "X" stared down into a countenance fundamentally weak. It was not the face of a habitual criminal. "X" recognized the man as Terry Rankin, a young man-about-town who had recently suffered heavy financial losses.

"X" lifted the unconscious man and returned him to the shadowy corner where he had been hiding. Then, the Agent entered the basement door, and proceeded down the dark flight of steps. He had decided that it was prudent to get the guard out of the way in case it became necessary for him to beat a hasty retreat.

Flashlight beaming ahead, "X" saw that the first room of the basement was evidently used only to store folding chairs which were sometimes set up in the hall when it was used for banquets and entertainments. Though his information was incomplete, "X" knew that if the poison gas was to be distributed throughout the building from the basement this could only be accomplished through the heating and ventilating system. Accordingly, he hurried down the concrete-lined corridor to a door at the end marked furnace.

In a chair that was tilted back against the wall, "X" saw an overall-clad form. A blue cap was tilted over the man's eyes, and he was apparently napping. As "X" approached on tiptoe, the man slowly raised his head.

"X" stopped. For beneath the shadow of the cap, was the broad, red face of Jim Hobart.

The private detective grinned, stood up, and touched the bill of his cap. "Mr. Pyke? I'm Jim Hobart. Mr. Martin was telling me I was to meet you here."

"How the devil did you get past the guard at the door?" Agent "X" asked, retaining the voice of Steve Pyke.

The private detective chuckled. "I walked in the front door, using my detective pass. Then I worked my way down to the basement where the custodian gave me a little trouble. I had to rap him over the head with one of his own pipe wrenches before he would listen to reason. I thought it might be better if I switched clothes with him."

"Good work!" Agent "X" commended. "You've been in the furnace room? See anything that looks like it might have the making of carbon monoxide?"

"Monoxide!" Hobart exclaimed. "I did see some odd looking cylinders in there. They're all connected with tubing. I thought it was a part of the regular air conditioning system."

"It'll condition the air, right enough!" declared "X" grimly. "It'll fill that hall above with corpses! This is a corpse-gang stunt, Hobart. It's up to you and me to save those people upstairs. That hall will be crammed with a thousand or more guests and police. The leader of the gang had the nerve to warn the police. He's out to run up another big record as the world's greatest butcher. Let's go, Jim!"

"X" pushed open the door, and led the way into the furnace room. The room was dimly lighted. Three great furnaces, hundreds of crossing pipes, large tanks, and electrically driven stoker cast weird shadows on the dull gray walls, and rendered a vast room seemingly small.

"Wait!" Secret Agent "X" held up a cautioning hand. He felt Hobart's fingers close upon his arm. "Footsteps, Hobart, scuffing on the other side of that door. Get behind one of those tanks. Wait till I call you."

"Right!" The blue-overall-clad figure moved like a shadow across the room. "X" stood perfectly still, his hand on the butt of his gas pistol. The door knob turned; the door swung slowly on its hinges. Outside, the hall was dark, but a darker shadow moved through the gloom. Only a pair of eyes were visible, gleaming through a shroud of black. The leader of the corpse-criminals seemed to float into the room.

"Everything is ready," came a husky whisper from behind the shroud. "The room above is crowded with guests and police. Turn on the gas, Pyke. You will find the valve just ahead of the manifold of the air conditioner."

Without a word, Agent "X" sprang toward the somber figure. His gas gun leaped from his pocket. "One move and you're dead! Here, Hobart!"

Jim Hobart sprang from his hiding place, an automatic in his hand.

"Cover this man, Jim," Agent "X" ordered.

Hobart needed no urging. The eye of his automatic was fastened on the black-robed figure. Still holding his gas gun, "X" strode to the shrouded one. With a quick, snatching motion, he untied the cord that held the shroud, and yanked the garment aside.

For the first time in his career, surprise rendered the Secret Agent unable to move. For beneath the shroud, contrary to all conclusions that "X" had drawn, was the beautiful Felice Vincart. Her green eyes were as cold as the sea. On her scarlet lips was a smile that was like poisoned honey.

Not for a single moment had "X" suspected that the

wealthy, thrill-seeking Leopard Lady possessed the necessary intellect to guide the gang along its corpse-strewn road of crime. Spy; lovely pawn in the hands of the master she might be; but that she directed the malign forces of the corpse-gang was unthinkable.

"Drop that gun, Secret Agent 'X'!"

Warm breath forcibly exhaled fanned "X's" ear. He half turned his head to encounter the cold snout of an automatic pressed to his temple. He caught a glimpse of a red, grinning face — the face of Jim Hobart!

The Leopard Lady sprang toward "X." A blow from her small fist knocked the gas pistol from his fingers. For just a moment, Agent "X" had been dazed. He should have known! The master criminal who fought "X" with his own weapons had somehow managed to impersonate Jim Hobart.

"You're not Jim Hobart!" "X" said through clenched teeth.

The man with the gun still grinned. "And you'll not be Agent 'X' if you make the slightest move. You'll just be a thing."

"X" felt the Leopard Lady's slender hand pass through each pocket, stripping him of his equipment.

"You poor fool!" the man who looked like Hobart whispered. "At the robbery of the Krausman Store, you were singled out and so was Hobart. Evidently, he was an associate of yours. Since early morning, I have been in Hobart's office, impersonating him just as you might have done. I was waiting for a call from you. In this manner, I could learn your plans. See how simple it all is? Since that day when I found my son on a slab in the morgue, killed by police bullet, I have planned how I might have my revenge.

"He was killed by what men call an error. In my organization, there is no chance for error. Years I have practiced voice control until now I can imitate any male voice to perfection. Then I sought for a suitable disguise.

I found it. I created my own army — faces of the past worn by living men. Hidden behind the masks I have made, you would find not men of the criminal class, but men who have become discontented with the lot fate gave them — thrill-seekers, financial failures, men of brain and brawn. That is my army. And the police believed them corpses! The city was terrified!"

"So you are the leader of the gang," Secret Agent "X" whispered. "And the Leopard Lady was your spy. But what have you done with Jim Hobart?"

"Oh, yes, Hobart. Let me see. I believe I brought him over to this building when my men and I came disguised as plumbers to rig up this gas generating outfit. Hobart is upstairs somewhere, bound in a closet. But he will be able to breathe — breathe the odorless fumes of the carbon monoxide that at this very moment is being pumped into buildings by means of the blower of the air conditioner. He will die along with the police and thousands of others.

"And with you and Burks and Foster and scores of others out of my way, I will carve from the underworld a greater empire than Napoleon dreamed of. That will be my revenge on the law!"

Realizing that many lives depended upon him, "X" went into action without for a moment considering the risk he ran. Lightning lashing the storm cloud, a meteor streaking the sky, an arrow in its flight — such make suitable comparisons for the speed with which "X's" right arm moved. Before the criminal chief could squeeze the trigger of that gun, "X" had knocked up the barrel. The gun made no noise, for it was effectively silenced; but "X" heard the rattle of the shot among the pipes overhead. He ducked, drove his right shoulder straight into the criminal's midsection. The man was thrown off balance, but he still retained his gun.

"X" sprang past him, zigzagged toward the great tanks of monoxide. He leaped behind one, knowing well that neither the Leopard Lady nor the bogus Jim Hobart would dare to shoot him; for if a stray bullet were to pierce the base of one of those tanks, the invisible, odorless death would flow into the room. For a moment he looked upwards through the maze of pipes.

He saw the great pipe that led from the air conditioner blower; he saw the smaller pipe from the monoxide tanks feeding into it. Because the gas was heavier than air, he knew that the valve connecting the gas source with the blower would have to be lower than the tanks themselves. He ducked behind a furnace flue and saw just such a valve within an arm's length of where he stood. He reached for it, looking under the metal tank-brace of the gang chief.

"You fool!" shouted the man. "That is not the valve!"

A grim smile crossed the Agent's face. "Isn't it? If it were not the valve controlling the gas, you would have shot me immediately. You are much too clever to shoot now. A miss and your bullet would nick one of these death-laden pipes!" And while he was talking with the man who would have killed him, "X" was screwing the valve tightly shut.

In a moment of frenzied rage, the killer loosed a shot that by some miracle burned across the Agent's arm, and cleared the gas-filled pipes. "X" ducked behind a tank, turned, and almost bumped into the Leopard Lady.

The gun in the woman's hand nosed upwards. Her cruel, catlike eyes narrowed. "X" saw her finger constricting on the trigger. But in that moment that he looked down at the gun, he learned something that the Leopard Lady did not know. What appeared to be a deadly automatic was in reality the Agent's gas pistol. "X" drew a deep breath and held it.

Felice Vincart would have killed without mercy. She was even smiling faintly at the moment that the gun in her hands hissed. The anesthetizing gas jetted into "X's" face; but instead of gasping it in, he exhaled with all his strength. Most of the vapor was blown back, directly into the Leopard Lady's face. For a fraction of a second, her face registered surprise. Then, she suddenly went limp; her cat-green eyes closed, and she keeled over backwards.

"X" hurdled the woman's form and saw, behind one of the furnaces, a possible exit from the maze of pipes and tanks. His work was not half completed. He might have checked the monoxide gas — if it had not already done its sinister work — but he had not stopped the criminal invasion of Memorial Hall. He knew that if life remained in anyone on the floor above, the corpse-gang would riddle men and women with bullets.

But as he rounded the furnace, he came face to face with the arch criminal. Both were surprised. The criminal's gun popped. A slug drove into the Agent's side with the kick of a mule. His bulletproof vest stopped the shot, but the fearful impact made him wince with pain. He led a terrific right that pounded into the killer's middle. The man doubled, head coming forward to meet the Agent's left hook to the temple. The man jackknifed to the floor, and lay still.

"X" hurdled the unconscious killer, raced behind the next furnace, and sprang into the open. He ran across the room, and yanked open a door that led to a stairway.

He bounded up the stair, thankful that above he could still hear the rumble of the crowd. He might yet be in time.

# XI

## THE BARGAIN

AT the top of the steps, "X" encountered a locked door. He pounded furiously upon it. It opened. The Agent dove headlong into the arms of Inspector Burks. Burks grappled with him, and, as "X" showed considerably more strength than Burks had anticipated, the inspector bellowed for assistance.

In another moment, "X" was surrounded by police. His arms were pinned to his sides. He was as near helpless as he had ever been.

"Well, well, well!" Burks rumbled. "It's Steve Pyke. Thought you were the man who was going straight. You picked a great place for a comeback, Pyke. You'd better think twice before you lay a hand on this stuff."

Over Burks' shoulder, "X" looked across the room. Near the ventilators in the wall, several men and women were lying on the floor. Others were bending anxiously over them. The carbon monoxide had been sufficient in quantity to attack those nearest its source. In glass cases arranged in rows across the great hall, "X" saw the priceless treasures of Kiev gleaming in the brilliant light.

"Inspector Burks! Listen to me!" Secret Agent "X" shouted. His voice had the swaying power of a master orator. "It is imperative that you get those people who have already succumbed, to the fresh air. Carbon monoxide has been piped into the ventilating system. It's a trick of the corpse-gang. They will be here to a man any moment. Everything depends on how quickly you act."

"Listen to him!" Burks scoffed. "You'll not talk your way out of this, Steve Pyke. Better slip on these cuffs before we force 'em on."

Across the room, "X" saw Commissioner Foster approaching the group of police. The commissioner had a worried look on his fine, strong face.

"Foster!" the Agent shouted. "May I speak with you alone?"

"It's Steve Pyke," Burks explained. "He's trying to pull something, commissioner."

Suddenly, "X's" right arm broke free from the man who held it. He swung a wide haymaker that sent the man sprawling back against his companions. With a mighty effort, he pulled away, dragging with him three surprised police who clung to his legs and one arm.

He reached the commissioner. His hand dropped on Foster's shoulder. His hypnotic, steely eyes drilled Foster's brain. "Unless you act immediately, commissioner, the lives of every person in this room may rest upon your conscience! I must speak with you alone!"

Foster's brow furrowed. He made his decision quickly. "Very well. Follow me. Inspector Burks, follow this man. Keep him covered with your gun."

Foster led across the hall to a small room at the side. "X" backed to the door and raised his hands above his head. "You may search me, inspector."

Burks passed his hands hurriedly over "X." "Picked clean," he grumbled. "Guess he's safe, commissioner, I'll be right out here."

Foster nodded, opened the door, and motioned "X" to enter. Face pale, lips stern, the commissioner followed.

"Foster," said "X" as soon as the door was closed, "the corpse-gang will be here any moment."

The commissioner nodded. "We have been warned."

"Believe me, Foster, this is no hoax!" said "X" earnestly. "Those people out there by this time should have fallen under the influence of poisonous gas liberated through the air conditioners. But when the gang arrives to find their leader has failed them, do you think they will turn and run? Certainly. But they will shoot their way out. Many innocent men and women may fall under their fire. If you will force everyone from this building or into other rooms, you and your men may lie in wait for the criminals, using the Kiev treasure for bait. The gang will enter unsuspectingly, and you will probably manage to capture the entire crew without the loss of a man."

Foster showed little enthusiasm for the Agent's plan. "It all sounds rather fantastic to me," he said.

"Do you honestly think I am lying?" "X" pleaded.

"Steve Pyke never told the truth," said Foster coldly.

"X" stiffened. His hand passed over his face. It seemed but a mere gesture; yet in that gesture, "X's" skillful fingers had altered the entire expression of his face. His nose was broad and crooked instead of thin. His chin jutted farther out. "Now, do you know who I am? I am the man who once saved your life. If you owe nothing to those people out there, surely you owe me something. Commissioner Foster, I am Secret Agent 'X'!"

Foster drew a deep breath. His face held a worried expression. Before him stood the man who was thought to be the law's deadliest foe. Yet Foster could not deny that "X" had saved his life.

"If I agree to permit you to handcuff me, will you act upon the instructions I have given you? And will you, in addition, search the closets of this building and liberate a deserving young detective by the name of Jim Hobart who was captured by the gang? Think; you will have nothing on your conscience. You will have saved thousands of lives; you will have captured Secret Agent 'X'."

Foster moved quickly. Handcuffs came jingling from his pocket. He took "X's" arm, and led him across the room to where a grand piano stood. He slipped one of the steel bracelets around one of the turned legs and locked it in place. It could be moved neither up nor down. He turned to the Agent. "I agree," he said. "Your hand, please."

Mutely, Agent "X" extended his right hand. He had

driven a bargain that might well mean the loss of his life; for the police were convinced that he was the most dangerous man alive. But to save the lives of those men and women in the hall, he was willing to make such a sacrifice — if it was necessary.

But as Foster clipped the cuff over the Agent's wrist, "X" expanded that wrist by muscular tension. He had agreed only to be handcuffed. By a clever feat, he would be able to compress the joints of hand and wrist; he would be able to slip from that cuff as soon as Foster was out of the room.

But no sooner was the cuff in place, than the door burst open. Inspector Burks strode into the room. "Sorry to listen to your confab, commissioner," he said. "You go out and herd the people into the upstairs. Maybe this guy's tip was okay, but the handcuff business was a phony. If he's the man he says he is, handcuffs don't mean anything — not unless you fix them the way I'm going to now![14]

"Very well, Burks. I don't know exactly what you mean, but I leave you in charge of the prisoner." Foster hurried across the room, through the open door, and closed it behind him.

"Now, Agent 'X'!" Burks was completely triumphant. He dropped on his knees. Both of his hands closed on the bracelet about "X's" right wrist. The Inspector's beefy strength forced the ratchet jaws of the cuff tighter and tighter until they bit deeply into "X's" flesh. Suddenly, "X's" left arm whipped up behind Burks' head and

---

[14] AUTHOR'S NOTE: Regular followers of the chronicles of Agent "X" will remember that he has used this handcuff escape, taught him by a Hindu fakir, a number of times. Inspector Burks had witnessed just such a trick when "X" escaped from him before.

crooked around the inspector's neck. His powerful muscles constricted, drawing Burks' head closer to his own. Great veins swelled on Burks' face. For the first time in his life, he knew what it would be like to have his neck broken.

The Agent's chin pressed against the bridge of Burks' nose. The pressure of that powerful left arm increased steadily, concentrating upon a particular nerve center at the base of Burks' brain. For "X," master of jiujitsu, knew every paralyzing hold in the category of the great Oriental system of defense. Burks' eyelids fluttered. His eyes protruded. He became limp and unconscious so suddenly that for a moment, "X" was afraid that he had killed him. But no, Burks was quite alive, though unconscious and gasping.

"X" released his grip. With his left hand, he frisked Burks' garments and produced a small key. This he inserted in the lock of the handcuffs. The jaws sprang apart. "X" took but a moment to handcuff the unconscious inspector to the leg of the piano. Then he was on his feet, running toward the door at the end of the room. He was not certain where it led, but he knew he must avoid the police at all costs.

THE door opened on a corridor that circumscribed the building. Ahead of him were stairs leading down into the basement. As he descended these steps, he heard the bark of an automatic inside the great hall. For a moment, he feared that the corpse-gang had entered before Foster had organized his ambush. He paused on the steps only long enough to hear the commissioner shouting:

"Put up your hands! Drop those guns! You are surrounded!"

Certain that the police had succeeded in cornering the criminal mob, "X" leaped on down the steps. The body of the gang might be in the clutch of the law, but while the master criminal remained at large not a person in the city was safe. "X" hoped that his blow to the gang leader's head had kept the man unconscious. He was loath to have the criminal fall into the hands of the police; for to Agent "X," the shrouded one was the most dangerous man in the world. He alone was in possession of "X's" secret.

"X" crossed a large recreation room in the basement of the building, entered a corridor, and hurried toward the furnace room. Inside the room, the dim light was still burning. Except for the hollow thud of many feet on the floor above, the room was sinister in its deathly silence.

"X" hurried behind the row of furnaces. The Leopard Lady lay where he had left her. But the master criminal was gone.

Had the man made good his escape or had he adopted another disguise in order to mingle with the crowd? "X" was inclined to believe that the man would try to get clear of the hall as soon as he discovered that his plan had failed. He would not have changed his disguise; for though the gang chief seemed to have limitless possibilities for vocal impersonation, his facial disguise depended upon masks. Such masks would be somewhat difficult to carry secretly.

"X" left the Leopard Lady there to be captured by the police. Then he ran across the furnace room and into the hall beyond. He hurried toward the rear basement entrance. As he bounded up the steps, he heard the grind of a motor car starter. A powerful motor kicked over. Flinging through the door and into the court, "X" saw a long, black car rolling toward the alley. Even in the gloom, he recognized it as the same black roadster that had terrified the city and slaughtered members of the police force with its machine gun.

"X" spurted, taxing his muscles to the limit. The long car swept past him. He could see two figures crouched low in the seat. Corpses or living men? A lunge, backed by every ounce of his strength, sent him flying toward the passing car. His fingers clutched at the slippery rear deck, encountered the spare tire carrier. "X" was jerked off his feet and dragged along the pavement. But somehow, he regained his balance, and, as the car turned into the alley, he sprang onto the rear deck.

He dropped full length on the smooth, rounding surface. His right hand extended until his fingers closed over the back of the seat. He drew himself forward. The two occupants of the seat did not move. "X" tumbled forward into the lap of the passenger. Even through the cloth of the man's suit, he could feel the chill of hard, dead flesh.

# XII

## BATTLE OF THE TITANS

THE black mystery car slowed up in front of a high brick wall. Beyond the wall, "X" could see the old Georgian roof of the house it enclosed. Rusty iron gates creaked open at a touch from the mystery car's bumper. Gears shifted soundlessly by an unseen hand, and the car glided up an unkempt gravel drive, tall grass rustling against its running gear. Headlights flashing on the garage doors opened them. The garage was large enough for four cars, but the mystery car came to a stop just inside the doors. The garage doors closed magically.

"X" was out of the car before the motor stopped. He stood perfectly still, waited. A slight sound of a well-oiled mechanism in motion, then complete silence.

A smile played across the Agent's lips. He dropped flat on the floor and rolled beneath the car. Fortunately, his pen-flashlight had not been taken from him. He turned on the light and sent its beam up at the underside of the car. A small V-type engine was mounted over the front axle of the car; it could not have occupied more than a third of the length of the nose of the car.

Directly above "X's" head was a sliding steel plate. He moved it aside, revealing an opening — a means of entering a compartment hidden in the cowl of the car. As "X" had guessed, the car was actually driven by a man concealed beneath the cowl. The corpses had been placed in the seat simply to attract police bullets.

The mounted machine guns in the hands of the dead men were operated by remote control by the hidden driver beneath the cowl. An ingenious system of mirrors enabled the hidden driver to see clearly the road ahead and to the sides through the three cowl ventilators.

It was little wonder that the police had failed to stop the car. They had directed their shots toward the harmless corpses in the seat, when actually the killer was safely concealed in the armor-plate compartment beneath the cowl. The killer had ghoulishly robbed the grave of Slash Carmody and others to obtain the corpses which he used as decoys in the car.

Where he lay upon the floor, "X" was directly above a sliding steel plate in the floor of the garage. By means of this door, the killer had managed secret entrances into the mystery car. Probably his own men were under the impression that the mystery car was robot driven.

"X" rolled away from the sliding door, and pushed it open. A black hole yawned up at him, and he could smell the damp odor of earth. Without hesitation, "X" dropped into the pit below. This was evidently a passage similar to the one "X" had explored when he had visited the Pyke house.

Suddenly, "X's" keen ears heard a sound of heavy breathing. His hands struck out, encountered a tightly drawn piece of wire. Instantly, the tunnel was lighted. Forty feet ahead of him, stood a man — a man whose face was the replica of Jim Hobart's. He seemed to have no sort of weapon. He was simply leaning on a crude wooden lever that stuck out of the wooden floor. His shoulders shook with silent laughter.

"People who don't know this passage generally get tangled up in my burglar alarm system," he said. "This place, Agent 'X,' is my last stand against the police — and against you. It has been carefully prepared to insure my security. For instance, I shall be forced to kill you in a few seconds. It shall be done quite simply, and in a manner that you will find quite unavoidable. You will be found by the police at a later date. I rather imagine they will be able to identify you — from your real face.

"As you may have imagined, I took an impression of your real face when you were unconscious and in my power. I made a perfect mask from your face in that plastic substance known as 'synthetic flesh.' That mask I have carefully hidden. As soon as you are dead, it will be turned over to the police. They will identify you from it. Agent 'X' will be pronounced dead. They will look no farther for the man behind the Corpse Legion."

"X" inched nearer the master criminal.

The man broke into a sardonic laugh. "No, no, Agent 'X." You cannot trick me. Were you to shoot me from where you stand, you would die the same way. Don't bother with trickery. It will avail you nothing."

Every muscle in the Agent's body was drawn tense. While the killer had been talking, he had advanced five feet. The man was still far away. Probably, he was armed, while the Agent had only his bare fists. He must entrust everything to his own agility and strength.

But even as the Agent sprang forward, the killer leaned full weight upon the lever in his hands. There was a deep, rumbling sound like a distant earthquake. Timbers in the walls and ceiling of the passage creaked, buckled. A beam fell across "X's" shoulders, knocking him to the floor. He struggled to rise, but at that moment, the sky seemed to fall upon him. An avalanche of earth and wood descended. Then all was smothered in blackness.

STUNNED, but only for a moment, "X" regained consciousness to find himself entombed alive. He was in a situation that would have driven another man stark mad; but "X" considered his position sanely, knowing that with only a limited supply of air, a few minutes of panic might be fatal. Though earth and timber covered him, it was not impossible to move. The beam that had fallen prematurely had struck him to the floor of the tunnel, but it had also fallen aslant of another wooden member. Now, that same beam supported the greater part of the wreckage and prevented the weight of the fallen structure from crushing him.

Opening his eyes, "X" found that a few starry points of light filtered through the debris only a few feet ahead of him. As he had dropped his flashlight when the tunnel had caved in, he was forced to work blindly. He pulled aside a splintered board in front of him, and wormed his way forward. Digging in the dirt, he dislodged another piece of wreckage and thrust it to one side. He pushed aside loose earth, and found that he was able to thrust his head through an opening. He saw that only that part of the tunnel in which he had been standing had collapsed.

Not far ahead, where the killer stood, the timbers were still sound. "X" realized that the gang leader, in constructing the tunnel, had concealed cables, levers and wires in such a manner that moving a single lever would release the whole flimsily constructed passage. This trap had not been particularly prepared for Agent "X," but was a simple means for the killer to burn his bridges behind him or bottle up his enemies in case of emergency.

It meant straining every muscle to the utmost; for once he had crawled from beneath the sheltering beam, he had to carry tremendous weight of the wreckage on his back. Fully ten minutes must have passed before "X" wormed clear of the pile of earth and wood and was able to stand upright. Ten minutes! His foe might have escaped in that time.

Agent "X" hurried, as quickly as caution would permit, up the passage to a rude flight of stairs at its terminal. He climbed the steps to bump against a round manhole cover set in the floor above. He raised it slowly and peered into a basement, evidently that of the old house which had been the destination of the mystery car. The room was dimly lighted and apparently deserted.

He pushed the iron manhole cover up farther, seized its rim to prevent it from falling back on the basement floor, and climbed through the opening. Quietly, he lowered the cover into place.

\* \* \*

THE room housed the furnace and coal bin. It was when he opened an unpainted door in the west wall that he made an important discovery. Precious as time was, he stood in the door staring about him. And from every conceivable inch of wall space, faces out of the past, faces of men long since dead, stared back at him with hollow, sightless eyes. They were masks that were perfect replicas of human faces. Beneath each one was a label. Near at hand, he saw the mask of "Big Tim" Riley, gang boss of prohibition days. Next to the Riley mask was another fashioned after the face of dead Willy Hymes. Everywhere were death masks, accurately tinted. This explained what "X" had long since guessed — that the corpse-gang was made up of living men wearing the faces of the dead.

"X's" eyes hurried about the room. He was hunting for one face that did not belong to a criminal. The future of Betty Dale depended upon him finding the mask that the gang leader had made in her image. Otherwise, she would eventually be hounded by the police. Only the mask of Betty Dale would prove to the police that she was not the person seen behind the mystery car's machine gun.

At the opposite end of the room, beside the one vacancy in the otherwise unbroken line of criminal death masks, he saw the lifelike features of Betty Dale. He hurried across the room and took the mask from the wall. It was made of very thin, flexible material — so flexible that when worn over the face, facial expressions on the mask were made possible by moving the muscles of the real face beneath.

"X" concealed the mask of Betty Dale beneath his coat, and was about to turn away when he noticed the vacancy on the wall near by. Two masks had hung there; the labels were still in place. One label read JIM HOBART. The other read THE REAL FACE OF SECRET AGENT "X."

So anxious had "X" been to find the mask that would clear Betty Dale, that he had forgotten for the moment that the master criminal was in possession of a record of the Agent's true features. He remembered the killer's threat — the police were to find the mask that recorded the real face of Agent "X" and they were to compare it with the real face of the man entombed in the passage below.

"X" sprang toward the door leading from the room. Perhaps he was already too late. Perhaps the master criminal had already sent the mask to the police.

From the next room, stairs extended up to the first floor of the house. "X" raced to the top and turned into a kitchen. From there, he cut across the dining room to come to a stop in front of a door leading from an old-fashioned reception hall. He stopped to listen. On the other side of that door, a voice was speaking:

"Hello, police headquarters. This is Dr. Jules Planchard speaking. I was kidnapped by the corpse-gang. I have just made my escape from the leader of the gang — the man called Secret Agent 'X.' I was pursued by this 'X' person when I ran through a passage leading from the garage to the house . . . Yes, I am certain that the man is Agent 'X.' I alone have seen his true face. What is more, I have a permanent record of that face — a mask made by the Agent himself. Death masks seem to be his hobby — masks of the persons he has impersonated. You will find the mask of "X's" true face in a Gladstone bag in the living room of the old Van Startz house. He was really quite an artist along that line . . . Yes, was. Agent 'X' is dead. You will find his body in the tunnel leading from the garage to the Van Startz house. The tunnel caved in while he was pursuing me.

Agent "X" tried the knob of the door. It was locked. His master keys had gone the way of his other special equipment. He backed away from the door, hunched his shoulders, and flung himself upon the panel. The lock burst. He catapulted into the room and sprang toward the desk where sat a man in blue overalls. "X's" right hand rammed into his empty coat pocket, his forefinger outthrust so that it appeared his coat pocket covered a gun.

"I have you covered!" he barked.

The man in blue overalls calmly pushed aside the telephone, and turned around. His breath hissed through the mask that cleverly counterfeited the face of Jim Hobart. "How unfortunate," he murmured softly. "How very unfortunate that you haven't got a gun. Really, you don't think I would have undertaken to impersonate you without learning something about your methods, do you? You have no liking for lethal weapons. Now, I have no foolish scruples about taking human life."

"Quite evident," replied the Agent.

The man at the desk laughed softly. He opened a drawer in the desk, calmly took out an automatic. "Do you happen to know who I am, Agent 'X'?"

"X" nodded. "I knew just as soon as I understood how the corpse-gang was created. No man in the country knows as much about criminal physiognomy as you do. You have had access to all police records. In the past, you have known every criminal who was impersonated by members of your gang. You have made death masks before!"

"X" took a step toward the desk. "Oddly enough," he continued, "the personal trait which told me who you were, you were unable to disguise by any mask. Perhaps, it is only a habit of yours that you have overlooked in your impersonations. Perhaps, it is a physical defect. The other night when we visited the Stinehope bank building, you found your opportunity to fade out.

"The raid on the Stinehope bank, you arranged ahead of time — just as soon as you learned that Foster and I were going to the bank. That raid had a double purpose. Not only did the gang manage to save the loot it had stored in the bank vault, but it gave you a chance to fade out of the picture. You wrote that note saying that Stinehope had been kidnapped, when actually —"

The killer's laugh broke through "X's" sentence. "So I am Stinehope!"

"Still trying to run a bluff?" asked "X" quietly.

The killer stood up and took a step toward "X." The automatic in his hand was unwavering. "Bluff? Of course, I'm bluffing. My entire life has been a bluff to hide my hatred of the law — and the men who represent it. Day after day I have schooled myself until I can impersonate any male voice. Then I sought for the perfect disguise. I was already skilled in the making of death masks. I needed something to produce practical masks as pliant as human flesh.

"Synthetic flesh solved my problem. Do you think I am after wealth? Only for what it can buy — the service of killers. I built up my army from the discontented victims of the depression and from groups of wealthy young thrill seekers. With my flexible masks, they were able to impersonate criminals who had long since died. I told them that the police would be too terrified to raise a hand against them. Actually, it was because of my machine gun bullets that the police had no opportunity to come in actual conflict with my men!

"I have killed over a hundred police, and my career is not yet finished. But yours, Agent 'X', has come to a definite end. And you will die without knowing who I really am!"

"X" held up his hand. "Never for a moment have I imagined you were Stinehope. Stinehope died the night your gang was forced to raid the Stinehope Bank in order to recover the loot. You were the first member of the gang to enter the bank that night. When you met Stinehope in the Krausman store that day, you immediately noticed that he was about your build and of the same blond complexion. Even then you must have planned that when you wanted to retire to safety, Stinehope would die and his body be panned off for yours.

"That night in the bank, you killed Stinehope after getting him to the top floor of the bank building. Then you came down to direct the activities of your men. I knew you were there. I did not see you, but I heard you breathe. It was that odd habit of yours of breathing forcefully in tense moments that gave you away.

"Then, as soon as you saw that Foster and I had a chance to escape, you went up the fire escape to the room where you had left Stinehope. You obliterated his features so that his body could not have been told from yours. You changed clothes with him. You wrote that note accounting for Stinehope's disappearance. Then you threw Stinehope out of the window. If you had only been able to work without breathing —"

The gun in the killer's hand jerked. A bullet sung past "X's" head. Another plumped into his chest and was stopped by the bulletproof vest he always wore. "X" hurled himself at the killer. His fingers caught the man's wrist. A quick wrench, and the gun spun across the floor. Then the murderer knew the might of Agent "X." He attempted to dig his nails into "X's" throat. "X" launched a terrific right that pounded into the killer's chest, driving out his breath and sending him toppling backwards to fold across the desk. His hands grasped thin air as he tried to struggle to his feet.

Then, a sudden, dull plop. "X" saw the killer's legs jerk. The man rolled from the desk, clutching at the front of his overalls. A dark stain was already spreading across the blue denim. He staggered backwards and collapsed on the floor.

"X" pivoted. Coming slowly across the room, dragging a rusty chain that was attached to his left leg, was a very dirty, very haggard Jules Planchard. The plastic surgeon stared dully at the man on the floor. The silenced gun drooped in his extended hand.

"Dead," he whispered like a man in a dream. "I have killed him. Weeks I have hunted the man who stole my formula for synthetic flesh. I had worked on it for years. It was the only artificial substance in the world that might have been grafted to living tissue. I had it nearly perfected. Then, he stole all my notes. Stole them through that damned woman I thought my friend — Felice Vincart. I should have killed her, too. The spy! Then he brought me here because he was afraid of me. He would have killed me had not Felice Vincart begged him not to. She loved me once — though she stole from me. But now — but now I have killed him!" His voice rose to an hysterical pitch. "I have killed him!"

Suddenly, the gun in the hands of Jules Planchard came up. He thrust the muzzle into his own mouth.

"Stop!" Secret Agent "X" sprang toward the crazed doctor. But before he could reach him, the gun had popped. Planchard fell forward on his face.

"X" stooped over the fallen doctor. He picked up the silenced automatic which had fallen from his hands after his suicide. He put the gun into his pocket, and went over to the desk. He took a piece of paper from the memo pad and scribbled a note. He removed the mask of Betty Dale from his coat and was placing it beside the note when he was suddenly aware of a harsh, familiar voice shouting in the next room.

For a moment, the Agent's heart stood still. He sprang to the door. Hand on the knob, he paused. In the room beyond, he distinctly heard the voice of Inspector Burks. Furthermore, he could make out the inspector's words:

"The telephone call referred to a black bag that contained the real face of Agent 'X'," Burks was saying. "This must be the one."

Agent "X" yanked the door open.

The silenced gun was in his hand. Burks and a plainclothes man were facing a small black traveling bag on the davenport in the living room. Burks' fingers were on the clasps!

Not for a fraction of a second did "X" hesitate. His future activities depended entirely upon the speed and accuracy of his movements. The silenced gun plopped once. It was a snap shot that nicked the handle of the black bag. Burks uttered a startled oath, and let it drop. He turned, snatching at his gun. But in the time required for Burks and his companion to turn, "X" had crossed the room to within a few feet of where they stood. Apparently, without aiming, "X" squeezed the trigger of the silenced gun a second time. Total darkness. The bullet had shattered the only light globe in the room

"The bag!" Burks shouted. "Grab the bag!" And Burks himself grasped at blackness, encountered a coat-sleeved arm, and hung on. He led a powerful right hook that landed. The arm in his hand went limp. A body sagged to the floor.

"Got him!" he shouted. "Lights, somebody!"

AS police burst through the French doors of the living room, flashlights lanced the gloom. Burks stared down at the man he had knocked out. It was one of his own detectives.

From out of nowhere, came a strange, eerie whistle. Burks sprang to the open front door. "This way!" he shouted. "Surround the house. Search the grounds!"

But his search was in vain. A few minutes later, a young detective came running excitedly to the inspector.

"He's dead!" shouted the man. "Secret Agent 'X' is dead!" He seized the inspector's arm and dragged him into the library where Planchard had committed murder and suicide.

"The guy with the mustache is Dr. Jules Planchard!" explained the young detective. "I remember seeing him in the papers. The other guy —"

"He looks exactly like that private dick, Hobart, we pulled out of the closet in Memorial Hall." Burks cut in.

"Looks that way," said the enthusiastic young detective. "But it's just a mask. Don't you get it? This guy must be Secret Agent 'X'!"

Burks knelt beside the corpse. With fingers that trembled with excitement, he lifted the flexible mask that covered the gang leader's face.

"Good Lord!" he breathed. "Why, he was supposed to be dead! Why, of all the fakes!" He gripped his companion's arm. "I begin to see! By heaven, no wonder he knew what all the oldtime criminals looked like. Why, he was a nut on making death masks of criminals, in the old days. When Foster hears this, it'll damn near kill him!"

"Who is it, inspector?" asked the young detective, leaning over Burks' shoulder.

"Who is it? Well, it's the ex-police commissioner of this city! It's Major Derrick himself! He retired several years ago when a policeman accidentally shot and killed his son. That must have been why he wanted to square things with the police!"

"But look at this mask on the desk," said another man. "It's the face of that girl reporter on the Herald!"

Burks strode to the desk, picked up the mask of Betty Dale and looked at it inside and out. Then he regarded the note which rested beside it. Aloud, he read:

"This will clear Betty Dale, won't it, Burks? In the basement of this house, you will find many masks of many people who are dead or alive. You will understand how Derrick created the corpse gang. Derrick used this mask to frame Betty Dale — probably because her father was on the police force when Derrick's son was killed. Sorry to deprive you of the pleasure of seeing my face. But look around you. Perhaps I am in this room right now!"

A tiny letter "X" was penciled at the bottom of the note.

Burks' eyes darted about the room. "Every man inside this room and close the door!" he ordered. "I'm going to see which of you has makeup on his face!"

The group of detectives looked at each other as though they thought Burks had suddenly lost his mind. And little wonder; for a mile or more away, one lonely man stood in a completely equipped scientific laboratory. It was a room known only to Secret Agent "X."

Light from the door of a small portable furnace cast strange, ruddy lights over the man's features — irregular and dirt smeared features they were, for the Agent's makeup had undergone considerable damage in the past thirty or forty minutes.

He stood perfectly still, fascinated by the flames inside the furnace. If one might have been permitted to look over the Agent's shoulder, one might have seen a strange thing in the heart of the flames. It was a little terrifying. Red and yellow tongues of fire licked up and around what appeared to be a human head — or at least a human face. The features were sagging, becoming more and more distorted as the flames devoured it.

But it was not a human head. It was only a mask, perfectly modeled after the true features of the living Secret Agent. No man would ever see the like again.

THE END

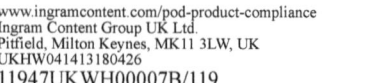
www.ingramcontent.com/pod-product-compliance
Ingram Content Group UK Ltd.
Pitfield, Milton Keynes, MK11 3LW, UK
UKHW041413180426
11947UKWH00007B/119